Pug and Joey N... dark and approached the Slipper cautiously.

Joey went into the saloon to make sure Kubik was there. And he was, behind the bar serving drinks.

"He's there," he told Pug. "What you gonna do?"

"He killed our man for the bank money he was carryin'. So we'll take that money away from him. We going to burn him out."

Joey was startled. "You do that and you'll burn down the town!"

"Izzit *your* town, kid?"

"No . . ."

"Then we'll burn it!"

WESLEY ELLIS

LONE STAR

AND THE TRAIL OF MURDER

JOVE BOOKS, NEW YORK

LONE STAR AND THE TRAIL OF MURDER

A Jove Book / published by arrangement with
the author

PRINTING HISTORY
Jove edition / December 1992

ISBN: 0-515-10998-3

Jove Books are published by The Berkley Publishing Group,
200 Madison Avenue, New York, New York 10016.
The name "JOVE" and the "J" logo
are trademarks belonging to Jove Publications, Inc.

PRINTED IN THE UNITED STATES OF AMERICA

10 9 8 7 6 5 4 3 2 1

LONE STAR

AND THE
TRAIL OF MURDER

★

Chapter 1

Jessie Starbuck was in Hatfield, a frontier town that was beginning to be an important center for the territory. She was sitting in the office of Daniel Oddum, president of the Hatfield Bank and Trust Company. Oddum had worked with her father; she remembered him from her girlhood, when he occasionally came to visit . . . because he always brought her a present, usually a doll.

Oddum was now a portly man in his sixties. His gray suit matched his hair and well-trimmed beard. His waistcoat was decorously flowered with a sparkling silver watch chain across it.

He had ordered tea and coffee and swept up papers and books as a clerk brought in a covered silver tray and placed it on the desk between Oddum and his guest. The clerk bowed to Jessie and hurried out, closing the door.

As the clerk left the office, three men came into the bank with drawn guns. They had wipes tied across their faces, and the leader said loudly, "Do as you're told and nobody gets hurt."

But one customer bolted for the door—and was clubbed viciously. He sprawled facedown and lay twitching for several minutes before he was still.

The other customers were herded into a room with the tellers and two women clerks. The three men began to fill the gray sacks they had brought with them. Then the leader noticed the neat placard on a door: Manager and President, Mr. Daniel Oddum.

He opened the door and motioned with the pistol. "You two—git on out here."

Oddum stood, flushing. "What is this!?"

"What the hell you think!?"

Oddum clawed a desk drawer open and grabbed at something inside—and the leader shot him twice. Oddum fell over his chair and dropped heavily to the floor.

"Git on out here, lady . . ."

Jessie was unarmed. She could do nothing else. She stepped out and saw at once that there were three of them, and one outside with the horses. She was shocked, seeing Oddum shot down—she knew he was dead; she had seen death often enough. She itched to do something about it, but they had the upper hand, so far.

One came from behind the tellers' cages with bulging sacks. He looked at Jessica. "You want t'put her with them others?"

The leader shook his head. "She's goin' with us." He took the sacks. "You go in and tell 'em—they foller us and we kill the woman."

Jessie offered no resistance, there being nothing she could do. Ki was at the hotel, a block away. He would find out very quickly what had happened and would come after her, but that would take a while. Her best bet was to act as if

2

she were helpless. They might expect that.

They rushed her outside to the horses. The street was quiet. Apparently the shots in the office had not been heard.

She was wearing jeans and a shirt and coat, her usual attire away from large cities. Her horse was in the hotel stable, but one of the men pointed to a sorrel and she mounted. They rode out of town, into the low hills.

There was no pursuit that she saw.

Ki was reading the weekly when he heard the shouting in the street. A boy ran into the hotel yelling, "They jus' robbed the bank!"

He rushed out and ran down the street. The town marshal, Leon Hacker, had just arrived, and his deputy was keeping the crowd back. He nodded at Ki and let him pass.

In the president's office, Hacker knelt by the body and glanced around at Ki. "Shot twice at close range." He stood and indicated the desk, where a drawer was open.

"Oddum prob'ly went for a gun and somebody shot him." He looked in the drawer and nodded. "They's a gun there. Goddamn dumb thing t'do, but he was a banker . . ."

Ki said, "He was with someone, probably Jessica. She said she was coming here." He pointed. "There's two cups and saucers." He glanced toward the other rooms. "Is she here?"

Hacker sighed. "They took her with them."

Ki swore.

A deputy brought one of the tellers to the office door. "This feller says they took Miz Starbuck with 'em and said they'd kill her if anyone followed them."

Ki frowned. "You heard them say that?"

The man nodded. "Yes. I brought that tray in just before the men came into the bank."

"Did anybody recognize any of them?"

3

"They were masked," the man said, shaking his head. "But I heard one call the leader Pug."

"Pug?"

Hacker said, "That could be Pug Bennett. Was he short, with red hair?"

"Yes, he was."

"He's a killer," Hacker said. "We got two killed right here. One shot and one clubbed to death." He took Ki aside. "You figger they'll carry out that threat to kill her if we form a posse?"

"That's impossible to guess—"

"*You're* going after them, aren't you?"

"Of course. But I'll go alone." Ki looked at the sky. "And right away."

He put some food into a sack, checked out of the hotel, and saddled his horse. Several sitters told him the four had gone south out of town, and he went that way. If they were holding Jessie as a hostage, they might not harm her, despite the threat. But what would they do later on? They would consider themselves safe from pursuit, but by then Jessie would know all their names. That worried him the most. Would they kill her to shut her mouth?

He wished he knew more about them.

According to the plain trail, they were heading southwest, following the stage road as the easiest track. He would have no trouble tracking five horses. Ki was a good tracker, maybe not nearly as good as some of the scouts hired by the army, but he could hardly lose a trail made by five horses.

Toward the end of the day, the tracks turned off the road and headed for a rise of low, wooded hills. Ki reined in and fished his binoculars out of the saddlebags to scan the hills. He could see no smoke or other evidence of them, but it was likely they were camped there.

If he crossed the flatlands to the hills now, while it was still light, and they had a lookout posted, they would know they had been followed.

He got down and waited till dark.

The leader had taken them out of town to the southwest, about ten miles along the stage road, then turned off it into some low hills. Jessie was satisfied they were leaving an easy trail. They had wound through the hills and beyond them, across a series of shallow ravines, and halted finally to make camp for the night in a large copse of pines.

The leader came to her. "We got to tie your hands and feet."

"I'd rather you didn't."

"Best tie 'er feet, Pug," one of the men said, but Pug ignored him.

"All right. You sit there and don't make no fuss."

Jessie did as she was told. So the leader's name was Pug. Another of the men was Bob, a much older man. The youngest was called Tipo—and that rang a bell. Pug and Tipo. She had seen those names on a Wanted dodger. Pug Bennett was wanted for murder. Tipo was wanted for robbery.

The fourth man was very quiet, hardly speaking at all. She did not hear his name mentioned till just before they turned in for the night. They called him "Windy".

Tipo gave her a plate of food and a tin cup of steaming coffee, saying he was sorry they did not have a chair and table for her. She thought he sounded sincere. When they turned in, he saw that she had a blanket.

Tipo was the only one who showed her any attention. Pug was deep in conversation with Bob most of the time. Windy was asleep or pretended to be.

5

She was able to sleep most of the night, knowing she would need her rest. She watched everything they did, looking for a way to escape, but they gave her no chance. Tipo slept near her—she suspected he had been detailed to keep his eye on her—and woke when she did. During the morning, as they saw to the horses and made breakfast, she felt his eyes on her. The others seemed to pay her no attention at all.

Tipo brought her a plate and coffee again, then joined the others as they talked out of her hearing. They were probably deciding their next move.

She thought about Ki. Was he on her trail?

It was full dark when Ki crossed the flatland to the low hills. As he approached them, he got down and led the horse, stopping to listen frequently, hearing nothing but the soft breeze.

He went through the hills cautiously, smelling for smoke, watching for a camp fire. He scouted ahead without the horse . . . They had gone through the hills and across a half dozen ravines and camped in a stand of trees.

He crawled near enough to smell the fire smoke and hear the murmur of voices, but he could not detect where Jessie was. When everything grew still, he crawled back to his horse and waited for dawn. With the binoculars, he saw them getting ready to leave, and Jessie was among them. He breathed a sigh of relief; she was obviously unharmed.

But she was sly.

When the four men and Jessie were out of sight, Ki followed cautiously, and came across a tiny bit of yellow paper. In the next mile he came across two more tiny torn bits.

Ki almost laughed aloud. Jessica was somehow managing to tear and drop them when no one was looking.

• • •

The first night, when she had curled in the blanket Tipo had given her, Jessica recalled the yellow telegraph form she had received from Daniel Oddum. It was called a flimsy, and she had folded it into her pocket and forgotten it.

In the morning, when they started out, she had torn off a tiny corner and dropped it for Ki to find. It was no trick at all to tear and drop the pieces. They expected nothing of the kind and did not watch her that closely. Not even Tipo had his eyes on her every second.

By nightfall she had refined her paper dropping. Where the five horses left a plain trail, she dropped none. But where the ground was hard, where Ki might miss the trail, she dropped enough.

Tipo often rode beside her and was full of chatter about places he'd been and music hall characters he'd seen. But he had never been east of Kansas City and was eager to hear about the really great cities such as New York and Boston; he had read about them in periodicals. Jessie answered his questions—it was a way to pass the time—and tried to find out from him where they were bound.

"To Berma," he said.

"Berma? What's that?"

"It's a town. You'll see."

"How far is it?"

"About another day's ride . . ."

"What kind of a town is it?"

Tipo grinned at her. "It's a town without no law."

★

Chapter 2

When he had found the bits of yellow paper and realized Jessie was dropping them, Ki was able to stay farther behind the outlaws, out of sight.

He had seen no evidence of a posse; perhaps Marshal Hacker had decided to respect the gang's threats that they would kill Jessica if a posse chased them. After all, the robbers had killed two persons in the bank. Why would they not shoot Jessie?

When the fugitives camped each night, Ki was able to creep very close—not close enough to reach Jessie, however. They kept her within their circle. He heard snatches of conversation, but unfortunately nothing he could use. They did not discuss their next move, for instance.

But he got close enough to see that she was unharmed. He wondered if they had ideas of ransoming her. Did they realize how much she would bring? Maybe not.

Three days out, he was sure they were heading for a

particular place; they seemed to know exactly where they were going—maybe to a hideout? Many outlaws, of course, had secret hiding places where they went to let things cool down after a spree. Then, when the law turned its attention to other matters, they would come out and commit more crimes or spend their fast-acquired money and plan other capers.

Tipo was exactly right. They came to Berma in late afternoon. It was a sprawling town in a narrow, forested valley that opened out to desert. It had obviously been there a long time. Many of the buildings were adobe with clapboard outbuildings and peeled pole corrals.

Jessie saw no women at all as they rode in. A dozen men stared at them; a few came out of stores to gawk at the newcomers, and the girl on the horse; she was something to see.

Pug halted and got down in front of a two-story building with a wide sign across the front in faded letters: COMMERCIAL HOUSE. He mounted the three steps up to the boardwalk and stamped his feet to get the dust off. He crooked his finger to her. "Come on, missy." To the others he said, "Put them horses in the stable." He went into the hotel.

Jessie was given a small room at the end of the second-floor hall. There were no back stairs. She had a chance to ask Pug, "Why did you bring me here?"

"Maybe you worth something." He grinned at her.

"You're going to sell me!?"

He shrugged. "That depends. If they ain't any market for you, then we can sell you to one o' the local folks. You ought to bring a hunnerd dollars."

"You're despicable!"

He laughed. "I dunno what that means."

They locked her in the room; she heard the turning of the

key with a heavy heart. Where was Ki? Would he find her in this place? If ever she'd needed him, it was now. She stood at the single window looking out at the distant foothills, which were striped with dark shadows and stands of pine. She had no illusions about what Pug meant. He would sell her to a brothel madam.

There must be a few of them in this hideout. Was it really a town without law? An outlaw town?

Ki approached the town late at night. He left his horse in the brush and walked in as if he belonged. There were few people on the street, and no one gave him a second glance.

There were three saloon–dance halls in the middle of town, all going full blast if judged by the noise. He saw two hotels, the Commercial House and a smaller one, the Berma Hotel.

The gang had the bank's money, so they were probably in the larger hotel, he thought. It doubtless had better accommodations, and it was in the center of town, near the dance halls. He was mildly surprised they had come here to a town as a hideout instead of a cave somewhere. There must be a reason.

He went back for his horse and then signed for a room at the Commercial House. None of the gang had seen him, and they wouldn't know him from Teddy's mule.

And if Jessie were here at the hotel, he might be able to figure a way to get her out of their keeping. What were their plans for her?

The hotel did not keep a register, only a kind of ledger, probably for the owner's benefit; he would want to know if he were making or losing money. Ki got a look at it, and there were no names, only dates and amounts. He did not have time to study it. He immediately went out to spend the night finding out as much information as he could.

For instance, he had wondered why the four men had come here and he quickly found out. It was an outlaw town. There was no law at all—except the word of a man called Luis Jagger, who, Ki had heard, owned half the town and employed a gang of toughs to keep the peace—and his grip on events.

Jagger had long ago put out the word that he liked quiet. So saloon shootings were at a minimum, since Jagger always ran out of town the man who pulled too many triggers. It was generally believed that Jagger feared the cavalry would one day come to bring law and order to Berma—if too many complaints were heard.

This ban on shooting was probably a pose, since Jagger did not hesitate to order his hired killers to do a job on any luckless pilgrim who happened to let the wrong people know he carried valuables. Such whispers had a way of reaching Jagger's big ears. Heeled pilgrims, minus the goods, were then carried feet-first to the local boot hill in plain pine boxes . . . which Jagger paid for. He got a special rate, along with the headboards.

Jagger was very greedy and suspicious. He was also paranoid, though he did not know the meaning of the word. He had a deep fear of prosecution, being well aware of his many crimes.

This suspicion made him leery of spies, and of anyone who was different.

And of course he quickly heard of the Chinaman who had just appeared in town asking questions. He might be a police spy. Probably was.

"Get rid of him," Jagger said. "Do it nice and easy."

Ki was sitting in the saloon next to the hotel as morning broke, hoping the four men would come in and give him a close-up look at them, when he became conscious that he was the object of stares. He got up and moved to

11

the back of the room, where there was a door to the privies outside. He sat at a table and fiddled with a deck of cards, wondering if he was about to be accosted.

Three big men followed him.

He saw instantly they were toughs, the kind he'd seen hired hundreds of times as bouncers. They swaggered to his table, one black-haired and ugly-looking, the others red-faced, one with pockmarks. They all wore pistols with knives stuck in their belts.

Black-hair said, "You—Chinaman. Git up."

Ki smiled at them. "What is it?"

"Git on yer feet!" They faced him across the table.

"Certainly," Ki said. He rose and suddenly exploded the cards in their faces. At the same time he upended the table, and the unexpected move tumbled one of them to the floor.

Ki jumped through the open door and slammed it behind him. He ran down the short hall, opened the outside door, and left it that way. Then he took the stairs to the second floor, hearing them shout and burst through the saloon door after him.

Pausing at the second floor, Ki listened. The three ran along the hall and outside—the door was standing open; he must have gone that way. Ki smiled. They would spend time searching through stables and outbuildings . . .

But why had they accosted him?

He looked along the hall. There were half a dozen closed doors. This was probably where the saloon girls brought their customers. He listened at several doors, hearing nothing. At another he heard the murmurs of conversation. It was early for the girls to be up and about; usually they were late risers, and it was still way before midday.

At the last door he heard nothing from inside and turned the knob. The door was unlocked. He slipped inside and closed it, shooting the bolt.

12

The bedsprings squeaked.

Ki looked at the bed, and a girl turned over and yawned then stared at him. "Who're you?"

He smiled, moved to the bed, and sat down on the edge. "Good morning."

"What're you doing here?"

"I'm sorry. Did I wake you?"

"I was just wakin' up." She frowned at him. "Did Doreen send you in here?"

"No. No, she didn't. I came by myself." She was a plain girl with hair all straggly; she looked to be twenty-five or so. She reached out for a comb on the side table.

"Are you a Chinaman?"

He smiled again. "No. Half-Japanese."

She looked at him curiously. "I never knew no Japanese people. There's some Chinese cooks in town . . ."

"Is that so?" he said politely.

She combed her hair, staring at him. "What *are* you doin' in here?"

"Well—the truth is, I'm hiding. Some men want to shoot me, I'm afraid. I'd rather they didn't."

"Jagger's men, huh . . . What'd you do?"

"Nothing—that I know about. Maybe they don't like strangers. I just got in town yesterday."

"Yeah. It's Luis Jagger. He don't like strangers."

"I've heard of him."

"He owns most of the town." She stretched her arms out, disregarding her nightdress, which was low cut, revealing the pink nipples of her breasts. "You can't stay in here." She swung out of bed and scratched herself. "If they catch you in my room they'll beat my ass."

Ki got up at once and went to the windows, looking down. The roof of the next building was just below. He opened the window and turned to smile at her.

13

"I'll go out here then. If they catch me, I won't tell them I saw you."

"Thanks." She joined him at the window. "One thing."

"What?"

"Don't trust nobody in this town."

"I won't. Will you close the window when I leave?"

"Yeah . . ."

Ki climbed out, smiled up at her, and hung by his hands.

It was only a short drop and he landed lightly. With a quick wave to the girl, he ran along the roof and climbed down on the alley side.

He was about a hundred yards from the trees. There was brush and grass in between. If he could reach the trees, he might be safe, but he'd have to run the hundred yards with no cover at all. Not good. The search was on now; he could hear men yelling to each other off to his right. He moved left along the back sides of the buildings on the alley path.

When he heard horsemen approaching, he slid into a privy and waited for them to go by. Had Jagger offered a prize for his neck? They must really be looking for him!

And they had to find him before nightfall or he'd get away in the dark. He wondered if the girl would keep the secret, or would she curry favor by telling them he'd been there? She'd probably keep her mouth shut. What good would it do them to know he'd been there?

He moved along the backs of the buildings—hoping no one would suddenly come out a back door—and came to what looked like a jail. It was a gray wall with bars and a barred jail door. It was leaning against a building with a huge rear door and a smaller one beside it. He realized it was a piece of scenery! Above the door was a sign: Berma Theater.

It was a playhouse!

14

At this time of day it should be empty and vacant. Ki tried both doors. Locked. But a side window was not. He pushed it up and squirmed in, then locked it. He was in a dark hall. He followed the hall and it came out on the stage. This was probably the way the actors got in; it probably led on the other end to a stage door.

He stepped out on the stage and looked at a sea of chairs. Everything was still as a tomb. Was there a caretaker?

There was barely enough filtered light to see his way. He investigated the backstage area and found a row of dressing rooms. There were cots in several and he considered lying down. But would the searchers come in? Why not? They might easily look into every building in town.

At the side of the stage, hidden by a heavy dark curtain, was a ladder. Ki went up it slowly and came to a three-foot-wide catwalk that crossed the stage, probably twenty feet up, with ropes for handholds. It was pitch dark. No one below on the stage could possibly see him—unless he also climbed the ladder.

He explored the catwalk and found he could get off it onto the back wall and climb in any of several directions if necessary. He would be able to hear anyone climbing the ladder—and see him probably. A searcher would bring a lantern. It ought to be easy to evade him.

He sat down on the catwalk to wait.

★

Chapter 3

The theater was well built, and Ki could hear nothing from the outside. Two hours dragged by. He lay on the catwalk, his eyes closed, holding the rope on either side. As he had been taught years before, he relaxed whenever possible, knowing he would be needing all his strength soon.

He dozed—and woke suddenly to a sharp noise. Someone had opened a door in the front of the theater. He heard voices.

Turning over on the catwalk, to lie on his belly, he saw men with lanterns come along the center aisle toward the stage. He counted seven; they climbed to the stage and stood directly under him.

"That damned Chinaman didn't get in here."

"Harry, try them doors—and the side windows too."

Ki heard fumbling; then Harry's voice yelled that the doors and all the windows were locked. "Nothin's been jimmied. He didn't git in here."

"Look into all them dressin' rooms . . ."

Ki watched them poke into the dark corners, but they seemed halfhearted. They were convinced he was not in the building. Several of the men said it was impossible.

"That goddam Chinaman can be gettin' away while we fritter time here."

Someone said, "Harry, better look on the roof too . . ."

"Yeah," Harry said.

They filed out, slamming the doors at the front, and all was silent again.

Ki waited a half hour, then got up and climbed down the ladder. In one of the dressing rooms he found a candle stuck in a bottle neck and lighted it. He flopped on a cot and sighed deeply.

Where was Jessie? He felt guilty running from his pursuers instead of protecting her. But of course if they grabbed him, he'd never be able to protect her in future.

He stared at the ceiling. Things were going to have to work out . . .

Jessie was locked in the hotel room, a tiny cubicle with but one window, facing rooftops and chimneys, with blue hills in the distance. The window, grimy and streaked, had been made so it did not open, and she could not see what was directly below it.

If she broke the glass, would she be able to get out that way? And if she broke it, would they hear it? The broken shards would fall to the ground outside.

And most important, if she broke the glass, it would have to be done in daylight so she could see what she was getting into—or falling into. For all she knew, there might be a lion chained under the window . . . or a nest of rattlers.

Where was Ki? Had he been able to track her to this place? So many questions . . .

She watched the sun go down; her tiny room became dark. They had left her a lantern, but no matches. Were they afraid she'd burn the hotel down—around her own ears?

Then, an hour or so after dark, a key turned in the lock and the door opened. Tipo grinned at her. He was carrying a cloth-covered tray.

"Grub," he said. "You hongry, missy?" He put the tray on the only chair and closed the door behind him.

Jessie stood with her back to the window. "Thanks." She watched him approach her, the sly grin still on his face.

"You don't look happy to see me."

She said with a touch of sarcasm, "I don't know why you would think that." She saw that it was lost on him.

He was within arm's reach of her and slowly put up one hand to rub her cheek. Then, in a lightning gesture, he grabbed the front of her shirt and tore it down to her waist. Her two lovely red-nippled breasts tumbled out as he laughed.

Jessie kicked out instantly, but he turned just enough, saving himself. He grabbed at her and flung her to the bunk bed. She let herself go limp, and as he dived at her, to hold her down, she swung at his head with all her strength, using her elbow—and connected. She heard something crack, and Tipo made a choking sound and fell to the floor, gasping.

Quickly she scooped up her coat and pulled at his belt, but he had come into the room without a pistol. Damn. She stepped over him to the door, closing it and locking it from the hall side.

She hurried down the hall to the stairs.

Voices. Men were coming up the stairs from the front! She ducked into an empty room and closed the door, leaving a crack. They went by and into a room farther down.

She slid out into the dark hall again and started down the stairs, watching below. No one was talking in the small lobby, no sounds at all, but the clerk was probably behind the desk and would certainly see her.

She crouched down below the railing as she came near the bottom steps. She could hear voices in the street. Men were likely to come into the hotel at any moment. She peeked over the rail. The clerk was sorting mail, putting it into various cubbyholes, his back mostly to her.

She crept around the newel post and gained the bottom hallway.

No one called out.

As she ran lightly to the back, she heard a crashing, smashing sound from the second floor. Tipo was probably kicking the door down.

But she was free—for the moment anyway!

As she gained the rear door, she heard Tipo's hoarse voice in the upper hall. He had gotten out of the room, and he would be snarly as a wounded cougar. She opened the door and slipped out, running to the stable.

But it would be the first place they'd look for her.

She ran through the stable to the alley and down it, wishing she had a gun. That would help the odds. Away from the hotel she slowed; anyone seeing her running would wonder why. She was far enough away now that anyone following her couldn't see her in the gloom. She paused, getting her breath. What was her next move? What would Ki expect her to do?

Get out of the town, probably.

There were plenty of saddled horses in the street, waiting patiently for their owners, who were probably in the saloons. Jessie hated to steal a horse, but this might easily be life or death—hers.

19

What time was it? She had no idea. But there were probably six or eight hours of darkness left . . .

Horsemen! Mounted men were coming along the alley toward her. Jessie ducked into a dark space between buildings and lay flat.

The riders went by at a walk, saying nothing. Jessie lay motionless, knowing they were searching with their eyes and would see the least movement.

But they passed by and she lifted her head, listening. By now, Pug would have the entire town roused, with Tipo wanting to slap her around. She'd have to get out as fast as she could, or she might never make it. She tied the scarf over her head; it would help conceal her blond hair.

She moved along the alley to the north, and once more horsemen entered ahead of her. She swung herself over a low fence, saying a prayer to Levi Strauss for the jeans she was wearing instead of a skirt. She remained still while the men went past, quicker this time, but more of them.

She slid back over the fence and continued. There were stables and corrals along the alley, but she wanted a saddled horse. She could easily find a horse in one of the stables, but the saddle and bridle might be impossible to locate without a light. She could not risk a light.

Many of the buildings on the main street had been built separately, as was usual, not sharing walls with one another, so there were spaces between them, some as much as twenty feet, mostly less. Jessica slid into one of these spaces and gained the street. To her right was a saloon with a dozen horses lined up at the hitchrack in front of it.

She peered about her, seeing no one moving close by. Farther down, a group of men were talking, standing in the middle of the street, a dark blot of them. And as she looked, several horsemen came from a side street and joined them.

20

To her left were more store buildings, then darkness. She was close to the north end of town.

She frowned and bit her lip, watching the men in the street. If they spotted her, they would probably investigate—everyone was now suspect of course. She could not enter a saloon, and all the stores were closed tight. By this time everyone in town must have been aware that she was a fugitive. Pug might even have offered a reward for her.

Might? He probably had.

★

Chapter 4

She needed one of those horses.

Bending double, keeping the horses between her and the dark knot of men, Jessie approached and selected a dun horse that had a blanket roll tied behind its cantle. There was even a Winchester there, in a scabbard. She smiled in the dark; this was the first horse she had ever stolen.

As she untied the reins from the hitchrack, a man came through the swinging doors of the saloon and walked directly to her. He was a youngish man, and she saw his brows rise as he looked at her. She was close enough that she saw recognition gather behind his eyes. He knew almost instantly who she was.

Her hand slid down to the rifle. She would not give up easily.

Then he smiled. "Don't worry. I'm not after you." He untied the reins of a bay horse and swung up, glancing at the men in the street. "Get on the horse and we'll ride out together."

Jessie slid her foot into the stirrup and swung up quickly. Before he'd shown up, she planned to lead the horse between the buildings, blending into the shadows, but this might be better. The men gabbing in the street would be on the lookout for one person. They might not try to stop two.

They moved north out of town side by side, at a walk. Her companion said, "Nice and easy does it. If we run, they'll chase us."

"Why are you doing this?"

He smiled, looking at her, showing perfect teeth. "I understand Pug Bennett has offered a reward for your capture—or for information about you. You *are* Jessie?"

"Yes, I am."

"Well, Pug and I are on the outs. It does my soul good to cause him trouble. I would be happy to throw him an anchor if he were going down for the third time."

She laughed shortly. "I see. Are you in his line of work?"

"I was once, a long time ago. But not now. Now I am a salesman."

"A salesman? Then what in the world are you doing in this town?"

He chuckled. "To save my neck. I will confess to you, I sell blue sky stocks—"

"Blue sky?"

"That means they are nothing but the paper they're printed on, no company, no mine . . . just paper. One of my disgruntled customers put out the word that he will pay five hundred dollars for my head, or for evidence of my passing, so I came here to let him cool off." He flashed the white teeth. "My name's Charlie, by the way."

"Charlie—what?"

"I don't really have a permanent last name. I've used so many in my business that I'm not sure what it was

23

originally. Just call me Charlie."

"Charlie, you are a crook."

"Yes, I know, my dear." He glanced back. "I think we're out of the woods, Miss Jessie. The town is well behind us. In which direction are you heading?"

"North . . ."

He nodded. "There're a dozen or more towns that way. Do you mind some company?"

She smiled. "As long as you don't try to sell me stock."

He held up his hand solemnly. "Promise."

Ki slid out of the theater the same way he had got in.

It was dark behind the building and he heard voices almost immediately. He lay flat, and three men walked past only a dozen feet away. One was talking about a girl he'd met in Pueblo last summer.

Ki got to his feet when they had passed, and slipped out to the main street. How far was he from the hotel where Jessie was held? He could not tell in the gloom. The street had no lights at all.

There were several knots of men moving and talking and Ki dared not go along the boardwalk. He'd be challenged for sure—and another chase would be on, one they might win.

He returned to the alley, ducking into a privy when mounted men came from the north end. When they had gone by, he hurried to the hotel and waited by the door till no one was in the small lobby.

The clerk on duty was a much older man with glasses and a bad cough. Ki walked in casually. "Is the girl still being held upstairs?"

The clerk stared at him in astonishment. "How you don't know about her?"

24

"Is she there?"

"Naw. She got out a long time ago. I thought ever'body knew it. Pug been tellin' ever'one about his reward."

"What reward?"

"A hundred dollars for information 'bout her. Where you been?" He squinted. "Say, you that Chinaman they lookin' for?"

"I'm not Chinese. Half-Japanese."

"Oh . . . izzat so."

"Where is Pug now, d'you know?"

The clerk shook his head. "No idea. I ain't seen him or the others since that girl got away."

"How'd she get away?"

"She locked Tipo into the room." The clerk laughed, then went into a coughing fit. When he came out of it, he said, "Dunno how she done it, but Tipo was mad as hell an' his face was bloody. That girl mus' be pretty goddam slippery."

Ki thanked the man and got out. So Jessie had slipped away from them. He stood in the deep shadows by the hotel and thought about it. Where would she be likely to go? She did not know for sure that he was on her trail . . .

She might head back to Hatfield.

Certainly she would not try to capture four desperate men. And they would be after her with a vengeance. Maybe they had driven her out into the desert. It was frustrating not knowing.

He could be positive the hotel clerk would tell Pug or anyone else that he'd seen the elusive Oriental. Ki knew he had to stay free if he were to help Jessie . . . but what to do?

He came to the same conclusion that Jessica had before him. He had to get out of town while they were looking

25

for him. He went to the hotel stable where he had previously left his horse, saddled up—the stableboy was nowhere around—and rode out.

But he had gone only a short way before a voice called to him suddenly out of the dark. "Izzat you, Bert?"

"Yeah," Ki said, hoping he sounded like Bert—whoever he was. The voice belonged to one of three men who came from his right.

He heard one of them say, "That ain't Bert!" Then one fired at him.

Ki dug in the spurs, and the startled animal dashed down the dark alley in a flat-out run. Bullets cracked by him, and the three yelled, emptying their pistols.

At the first cross street, Ki turned right, and it petered out in a hundred yards; he was in the trees. He reined in quickly to walk the roan. It was dark as the inside of a raccoon. His pursuers had stopped shooting, but they still yelled, telling others they had seen the Chinaman.

He walked the horse slowly, fearful of stumbling over fallen trees. He turned left, hearing the growing ruckus behind him. Someone was shouting to spread out. Ki rode just within the fringe of trees, the town on his left. It sounded like ten men had gathered to chase him. A hundred dollars was a lot of money.

They would probably expect him to put as much distance between them as he could. Instead, he circled back into the town.

He crossed the main street, walking the horse easy, and headed west. It would be dark for another five or six hours, and at the moment dark was his best friend. He met no one as he left the town behind and turned north.

Go north, Jessie . . .

★

Chapter 5

They were well away from the town and were not being followed. Jessie and Charlie made certain of that by laying in wait, watching their backtrail. Only a few rabbits and a deer showed up.

Satisfied, they went on, easing the pace. Jessie worried that she should go back to search for Ki. It was hard to know what to do when she did not know if he had been able to track her—maybe the wind had blown the bits of yellow paper away.

She said nothing of this to Charlie. He was a charming sort; of course charm was his stock in trade. He did not impress her as being overly resourceful—as Ki was. Charlie would undoubtedly take the course of least resistance when the chips were down.

But there was no doubt he was pleasant to be with, and she enjoyed his company. He kept up a chatter, telling her of his flimflam adventures, many of the stories funny at his own expense. He was able to laugh at himself more than anyone she had met.

Of course he was a crook. He showed her beautifully engraved stock certificates, on excellent paper; they looked very impressive. They were of companies that did not exist except on his paper; they were mining and oil stocks in various denominations printed in both blue and gray inks.

He swore to her he never harmed anyone, except a bit financially. He never sold to widows or those who could not afford to lose the money. Jessie sighed inwardly, wondering what his oaths were worth. Such a man was undoubtedly a magnificent and accomplished liar.

But he did make it all sound so very convincing. And he had a wonderful open smile. Looking at his teeth, she thought of the tiger about to chomp down on a lamb.

However, he had helped her get out of the outlaw town. That could not be denied. She might have done it alone—might have, but she would probably have been pursued with impossible-to-know results. Charlie had done it smoothly.

On the second day they came to a region of tree-covered hills and followed a chattering stream to a tiny valley where a shimmering pond had formed. It was a warm day with a sighing of breeze overhead, roving the treetops.

Charlie reined in, gazing at the blue-green water. He grinned at her. "Looks like a bath, don't it?"

Jessie nodded. She would love a bath! Just ahead was a tawny meadow with clusters of red willow along the shoreline.

Charlie gestured to a point of land that jutted into the pond, where the trees came down to the water's edge. "You go up there and have your bath. I'll stay here. D'you have any soap?"

"I think there's some in my pack . . ."

"Good. I'm sure I have some too." He slid off his horse and hobbled them both in the meadow grass.

Jessie walked out to the point of land. The water looked very deep here, close by the shore, very deep and green. She could see small fish darting about as her shadow fell on the water.

Glancing at Charlie, she pulled off her boots and struggled out of the tight jeans. Then the undershirt and soft outer shirt. She hung the clothes on a stout willow thicket and tested the water with a bare toe. It was cool but not chilly.

She let herself down into the water, sucking in her breath at the first cold bath of it. She swam a few yards and came back for the cake of soap. And as she began to soap her shoulders, Charlie appeared, swimming easily, grinning at her.

"I was wrong," he said. "I don't have any soap. Maybe I can borrow some from you."

She knew instantly that whether he had any or not, he would have come here. She could tell him to swim back— but was it her lake?

She tossed him the soap and he smiled, catching it deftly. He came close. "Let me soap your back . . ."

She turned and felt his hands on her white shoulders. For several moments he worked diligently with the soap.

And then she felt his erection. It pressed against her backside for a moment, then moved away—then came again, sliding across her buttocks. Jessie closed her eyes; it had been a long while since a man had caressed her. She stood on the sandy slope of the pool and felt herself relax. His hands moved down her back to her round bottom. Then they came around her, moving across her breasts, then away, and the rampant member nestled against her backside.

He was very gentle with her, rubbing smoothly with the bar of soap—and then there was no soap; his hands were caressing her, fondling her hard-nippled breasts, sliding down over her belly and back again.

Her heart was pounding and she leaned against him. Her hand touched his hard maleness, and she grasped it, squeezing and moving on it. How strong it was!

Charlie kissed her neck and her cheek, holding her tightly. She turned her head and their lips met. One hand slid up between her thighs, and she moaned softly, rubbing the erection on her thigh as his fingers made electric contact.

He turned her toward him and they kissed again. She lifted her leg and the hard member slid against her, causing her to shudder and slide the leg around him.

She felt it come into her a bit, and she pressed herself against it, wanting it . . .

Then he lifted her and carried her to the bank. He put her down on the grass, kissing her softly. She pulled him down and he was pressing into her . . . She lifted her knees, feeling the invader come in deep and warm . . .

His arms held her and she smiled, gazing at the saffron sky over his shoulder as he stroked her . . .

Ki was of two minds about leaving Berma. He wanted to bring Pug Bennett to justice—somehow—but he also had to find Jessie. And of the two, Jessie came first. Jessie would always come first.

But where was she?

Possibly putting miles between her and the town, if the clerk could be believed. Was she alone or being chased or followed? If she were alone, she might well be heading for Hatfield. If she were being chased, she might go any direction to escape.

It seemed he had only one option. Go toward Hatfield.

• • •

Pug Bennett hated the nickname; his given name was Judson. How he had acquired the "Pug" he really did not know. It had been hung on him as a very young boy, and he'd never been able to get rid of it. He answered to it because very few knew his proper name and he was tired of explaining.

He had put Tipo in charge of the girl, wondering how long it would take him to tear her clothes off. He had been slightly surprised that Tipo had gotten this far. Maybe Tipo was not as woman-crazy as he led people to believe.

His threats, back in Hatfield, had apparently kept a posse off their necks, but now the girl had come to the end of her usefulness. They didn't need her anymore. And she knew all their names and could describe them.

It was time to do away with her.

He called Bob in and told him to get Tipo. The two of them were to take the girl out of town somewhere, in a lonely spot, and bury her where the body would never be found.

Hearing this, Bob grinned. It meant they could do anything with the girl they wanted—before they buried her.

Bob went up to the room and came down in a hurry to yell at Pug. The girl had escaped!

Pug swore in two languages and demanded they find her and shoot her on the spot! Where the hell was Tipo?

They were unable to find her.

It had been dark when she broke out of the hotel room and disappeared. The hotel clerk swore he had not left his desk; the stairs were in plain view. Thereupon Bob and Windy searched the entire second floor. They went into every room, occupied or not.

She was not in the building.

She had fractured Tipo's jaw and it hurt like blue blazes. Tipo swore she had hit him with a heavy chair leg. He had

31

routed out a doc to have the jaw treated and now wore a heavy white bandage.

Bob and Windy spread the reward offer—one hundred dollars for any news of her.

No one came forward.

She had dissolved into nothing, disappeared completely. And daylight was no help. Pug got men busy searching every building in town without results. Luis Jagger helped, having his own men search.

They turned up one fact: two horses were missing. Their owners said they'd been tied in front of the Senate Saloon, and now they were gone. One had probably been stolen by the girl, the other maybe by the Chinaman they pursued. Did the two know each other?

Yes. The hotel clerk reported that the Chinaman—who was not Chinese but Japanese—had asked about the girl.

Very curious.

There were tracks everywhere of course, close in around the town; they were no help. There was only one road leading into Berma and out of it, mostly used for hauling supplies to the various stores and saloons. It ran east and west, and a child could plainly see that no one had used it for days.

Tracks were spotted leading north, and since the girl had been taken from Hatfield in the north, she might be heading back that way.

Pug thought so.

Charlie was bound for a much larger town than Hatfield, he said. It was not gainful as a rule, and might easily be life-threatening, to sell worthless stocks in a small town where unhappy buyers would know where to find the seller. The thing to do, Charlie said, was to sell and get out of the neighborhood fast. A big town had lots of neighborhoods.

But he would accompany Jessie as far as Hatfield, and was delighted to do it. He knew Pug Bennett from years past and described him as a ruthless killer who would stop at nothing to get what he wanted . . . usually money. He was also a backshooter and a liar, and Jessie was fortunate to have busted out of the hotel when she did.

"If I hadn't," she replied, "I wouldn't have met you."

"Your luck is running strong," he agreed gravely. "Who is this person, Ki, you mentioned?"

She explained, saying she was sure Ki had tracked her to Berma. "He's probably looking for me this minute."

"Then we're in trouble. If we send up a smoke signal for Ki, we might very well draw Pug and his gang. And there're four of them."

"Do you think Pug will come after me because of the bank shooting?"

"In a second," he said. "You were a witness to a killing by him, weren't you?"

"Yes . . ."

"So you could be instrumental in seeing him hanged or at least put in prison for the rest of his life. I think he'll kill you if he can. It's Pug's solution to problems. In fact, I'm surprised he let you live as far as Berma. His mind must have been on other things."

"I stayed out of his sight as much as I could."

"That was wise."

They walked their horses through broken country; it was necessary much of the time to ride in single file. Charlie kept his rifle across his thighs, and Jessie checked the Winchester she'd acquired. It had a full magazine and seemed in good condition. She wished she had a chance to sight it in.

If they met Pug and his three, she and Charlie would be at a disadvantage in numbers, and they did not know the country. Maybe Pug didn't either . . . Charlie had been threatened many times, he told her, but had avoided trouble, usually by leaving the scene. It was a much better plan than fighting or staying where a stray bullet might find him.

That speech did not impress her. Would Charlie stand and fight if it came to it?

They were, she estimated, about a day's ride from Hatfield when they were attacked. They were in single file, with her in the lead, when the shots came seeking them.

Jessie spurred off the trail and slid down instantly, pulling Charlie off his horse.

He fired back at their pursuers as she tied the horses in a sheltered place, then climbed above them into the brush and rocks. Charlie came after, swearing under his breath.

"Izzat Pug shooting at us?" he demanded.

"Probably. They must have gotten around ahead of us." She indicated the rifle in his hands. "Can you use that?"

"Of course," he said stiffly. He looked around. "Where are they?"

She pointed. "Up there. Keep down low. They fired too quick and now it may take them a while to work around to another direction."

"You think they will?"

Jessie nodded. "They'll think they have us boxed in and that we'll retreat. Instead, we'll go forward. Come on."

They were on a rocky ridge that provided hundreds of hollows and masses of dusty brush cover. Jessie slid from one to the next. The sniper had fired from above them and had fired too fast and also downhill—which had helped him to miss. She guessed the shots had come from about a hundred yards distant. The trail she and Charlie had followed was an up-and-down affair so they'd probably only been in view now and then, for a few minutes.

She led across the ridge, keeping in the shadows whenever possible, beckoning Charlie to follow. When he caught up to her, he said, "What about the horses?"

"They're the least of our worries at the moment. We have to save our skins." She moved off. Charlie had probably never been in a fight before. She smiled to herself. He would remember her.

The others were doubtless moving too. She stayed high; it was always better to hold the high ground in a firefight—if possible. It put the enemy at a disadvantage. The first shots came from east of them, and the second from the north, three quick shots seeking them out. They spanged off the rocks, causing Charlie to gulp and swear.

When he saw her looking at him, he managed a weak smile. "You wanna buy some mining stock, lady?"

★

Chapter 6

Jessie laughed. At least he was putting up a brave front. She motioned him down when more shots came, striking the rocks around them. Ricochets whined harmlessly into the sky.

Jessie said, "They're hoping for a lucky hit, but their angle is wrong."

"How long will they keep this up?"

She gazed at him in surprise. "Until they shoot both of us."

He sighed deeply. "Can we get away?"

"We might, but it would be on foot. It's a long walk to Hatfield." She studied the sky. "It's about five hours till dark. We can try something then."

"Where are their horses?"

Jessie smiled. "Exactly what I was thinking." She nodded toward the east. "They're probably over there. We'll climb down this slope and around that far hill. Are you ready?"

"Let's go."

But as they started the move, more shots came, a deadly hail. The ambushers had spread out, and they were firing from widely scattered spots.

Jessie and Charlie lay behind the rocks and waited; how much ammunition did Pug and his gang have to waste?

When the barrage let up, Jessie pointed down the slope. She moved cautiously and Charlie followed. They gained the bottom of the slope and started around the brushy hill, climbing upward again. No more shots came after them. Possibly Pug and his men were climbing toward the spot where they'd been. She smiled. If they tried to come down the slope, they'd be in plain view, good targets.

She came out on a rounded ridge and lay flat, facing the way they'd come, waiting. When she saw movement on the opposite ridge, she fired, aiming carefully, then scurrying down. It was impossible to tell if she'd hit anything. But there was no return fire.

Charlie crawled over the ridge, panting. "What'll they do now?"

"Circle around to get at us—or wait for dark."

"Which?"

"I think they'll do something rather than sit and wait. But it'll take time. Let's see if we can find their horses."

Ki reined in, hearing the distant shots. He was in hilly country and his first thought was ambush. Pug Bennett and his uglies could be ahead of him—or the shots could have come from some bushwhacking highwayman, making a dollar off a pilgrim. But that last was unlikely, he thought. A robber would starve to death waiting for victims along this lonely trail.

He went forward cautiously, listening for the shots. Was Jessie close by? When he got closer, it seemed both parties were on opposite ridges. He halted, tied the horse, and continued on foot, touching the *shuriken* in his vest.

From the sounds, it seemed that only two people were on his right, and Jessie might very well be one of them. He left the trail and came into a tangle of brush and rocks—and found two tethered horses.

Without hesitation, Ki led the two horses back to his own mount. They could not belong to Pug; he had three men with him.

He gave the recognition whistle he and Jessie had used a hundred times—and received a reply. She *was* close by! He moved to the right with the horses and in a few minutes came upon her—and a stranger.

"This is Charlie," she said to Ki. "He helped me get away from Pug and his men."

They shook hands. "Delighted to meet you," Charlie said with a smile.

"And you," Ki replied politely.

Jessie was surprised to see their horses. She and Charlie had been about to go back for them. She explained to Ki that Pug and his men had tried to outflank them and had probably left their horses on this side of the hill.

"Then mount up," Ki said promptly. "Let's find them—and take them along with us."

Pug was in an ugly mood. He himself had fired the first shots and missed. He blamed the light and the winding trail; he'd only had a few seconds to aim . . . The two had ducked away instantly, and now it was necessary to flush them out of the rocks. Not an easy job.

There were only two of them, and one a girl. But obviously not an ordinary girl. She had given Tipo the slip and hurt him badly in the doing. Tipo naturally swore it was a lucky hit . . . Maybe. And now he growled that he would do unmentionable things to the girl when they caught her.

They shot at the two, keeping up a fire on the opposite ridge. Someone fired back very accurately, which did not help Pug's mood.

Firing back and forth would get them nowhere; they had to flank their prey. Maybe they could be caught in the open . . . but it did not happen.

Pug scowled at the sky; he did not want to wait for dark, not in this tangle of hills. He sent Windy and Bob in one direction, and he and Tipo went in the other; they closed in on the hill. It took a while, and when they got there, they found no one.

There were tracks down a slope, and they followed, spreading out again to come onto the second ridge from two sides—and find no one there either.

Pug swore a blue streak. How could anyone be so goddam elusive? They could find no tracks on the hard ground, and he growled, deciding to give it up. The two they pursued had doubtless hightailed it away like scared rabbits.

"Let's git back to the horses," Pug said.

But there were no horses.

Ki found the four mounts concealed in a coulee and led them out, grinning. With the horses in tow, he, Jessie, and Charlie hurried away toward Hatfield. Pug and his men had lost all the way around this time.

Ki considered an attempt to capture the gang, but both Jessie and Charlie were about out of ammunition and he had certain doubts about Charlie. He had performed well so far, Jessie said, taking Ki aside, but he was not a fighter and might let them down in a pinch. Pug and his men were experienced gunmen, after all.

Hatfield was closer by far than Berma, so the outlaws would probably go there for mounts.

When they reached the town, they left the four horses in a livery corral and went at once to the hotel.

Over supper, Ki and Jessie expressed their desire to round up the four outlaws and see them face a judge and jury for the murders and robbery. But Charlie wanted no part of it. When the meal was over, he bowed to Jessie, shook hands with Ki, and said he would be moving on in the early morning.

They wished him well. He had helped Jessie when she was in trouble—possibly one of the few decent things he had done in years, but he *had* done it.

When they talked to Marshal Leon Hacker, he was visibly nervous hearing about Pug and the three toughs coming into his town again. "I got only one deputy. We ain't no match for them."

"If they come," Ki said, "they'll come on foot and we ought to be able to grab them all. They'll be tired and hungry . . ."

Hacker said, "How can you be sure they'll come here?"

"Hatfield's the nearest town."

"Maybe so." Hacker made a face. "But it's been my experience that outlaws don't do what you expect. If they did, more of 'em would be in jail."

Ki agreed. "But it's our best plan at the moment. Can you get five or six men together to help out? We'll want a good show of force."

"Yes. You figger they'll go first to the stable?"

"It's a guess. They'll want horses. They've been here before, so they know where the stable is."

"And you also figger they want Jessie."

Ki shrugged. "She saw Pug murder the bank president."

Jessie spent time writing down all she could recall about the four outlaws, their names and descriptions, habits and any trivia she could remember. When she finished, she

40

stuffed it all into an envelope and sent it to the U.S. Marshal's office, eighty miles away. Let him decide his next move.

She did not mention Charlie.

Pug raged that the girl had gotten away. She was the one he cared about. She had seen him shoot the banker. He should have shot her then! It was always messy to leave important details like that in one's trail. You never knew when they would pop up to throttle you. He kicked himself for allowing Tipo to talk him out of finishing her off when they had her.

The Chinaman was less important, of course. He had seen nothing and was probably just a nobody anyhow.

When he discovered their horses had been taken, Pug had screamed and yelled, white with rage. He had never run into such a flood of bad luck! They were all afoot! Ever since the girl had escaped Tipo, things had gone sour.

It was some consolation to him that Tipo was in pain from the fracture. It hurt him to talk and eat, and several of his teeth were loose. Pug enjoyed seeing him wince and strain. It served him right.

Both Bob and Windy tried to talk him out of it, but Pug headed for Hatfield. He was adamant. The girl had to go.

Bob said, "They'll expect us, for crissakes." Windy agreed.

Pug growled. "They won't know when we'll show up."

"But they'll be watching."

"You don't know that."

"Forget that damned girl," Bob said. "You jus' want to go back to get rid of her."

Pug snarled at him. "It ain't smart not to."

★
Chapter 7

Their boots were not made for walking, and they did not cover the miles well. Their legs ached after the first day, causing them to stop frequently to rest. It took nearly three days to come in sight of Hatfield, the first sign of civilization they'd seen since Berma.

When they glimpsed the smoke in the distance, Pug halted. "We'll wait till dark."

Bob told him, "You got no idea where that girl is. What you gonna do about her?"

"I dunno yet. First, we git us some horses. Walkin' is for farmers."

But in this, wanting horses, Pug was predictable. The stable had been staked out, and when the outlaws appeared, dark shadows along the street, a half dozen townsmen opened up on them.

Ki had coached them carefully. "Wait for my signal."

But he might as well have been shouting into the wind.

Clerks and shopkeepers waited for nothing. They saw the quarry, and they fired as fast as they could pull triggers. They blasted the glass from three storefronts, brought down a shoemaker's sign—and killed Windy.

Pug and the others made their escape over fences and into the fields, losing themselves in the dark. Bob had several scratches, and Tipo, in the rear, was saved only by his rifle stock. It took a nasty hit, jerking him around. But he was unharmed except for minor bruises. Pug was untouched.

The ambush did not improve Pug's outlook.

"We was dumb," he said grumpily. "We shoulda knowed they'd be watchin'."

Bob said nothing but rolled his eyes.

Pug frowned at Tipo. "You sure Windy got it?"

"Positive," Tipo said. "He got a hole in his head. He come all this way to meet that goddam bullet."

"They was all shootin' high," Bob said. "Windy just run into bad luck." He looked at Pug. "Why can't we steal us some horses in town?"

"Yeah, we going to do that. But not all at once. We'll draw straws, see who goes in when."

Tipo asked, "How we going to know where the girl is?"

"Use our eyes, for crissakes! She can't stay cooped up forever, can she?"

Ki and Leon Hacker were annoyed that the ambush had gone so poorly. Ki had had hopes of bagging all of the outlaws. But they had gotten one; someone had drilled Windy through the temple. Hacker sent a boy for the undertaker and in the meantime went through the dead man's pockets. But there was nothing on him to say his name.

"They called him Windy," Jessie said. "I don't think I heard him speak four words."

The undertaker said, "I hate t'bury a man 'thout no name, even if he was a owlhoot."

"Call him a John Doe," Ki said. "He rode with the wrong crowd but the Almighty knows his name. Don't fret yourself about it."

"Yeah, ain't that the truth. All right, I'll plant him t'morra. Put up the headboard next week, soon's I get 'er painted." He climbed onto his wagon.

Back at his office, Hacker went through his files and found a Wanted dodger with Pug Bennett's picture on it. Wanted for murder in Missouri and Oklahoma.

"It's five'r six years old," Hacker told Ki. "He got a beard in the picture. Has he got one now?"

"No, just a mustache."

The Marshal pursed his lips. "There's a lad over to the newspaper who can paint out the beard. Then we can make copies."

Ki smiled. "Very good."

Hacker let no grass grow under his feet. He went to the newspaper office, talked to the owner, then stood by the desk as an artist painted out the beard, leaving only a mustache, on the photograph of Pug Bennett.

The printer was able to make him a dozen copies, and by nightfall Hacker had them all tacked up about town.

The newspaper was glad to print the picture with the caption "MURDERER!" and a biographical sketch of Judson—known as Pug—Bennett, listing his nefarious deeds, his prison stays, and the gang—Windy, Bob, and Tipo.

The rewards were also prominently featured.

"Other papers will pick it up," Hacker said. "We'll make it as hot as possible for the Bennett gang."

Pug was surprised and disgusted by the unexpected ambush, and by Windy's death on the street. He knew he'd been outsmarted, and it rankled. It was disturbing that a lawman should be able to get inside his head that way and outguess him. Or was it just dumb luck?

Maybe . . . it could have been luck . . .

He was aware that he and the others should depart for far parts, possibly Oklahoma Territory, and lie low for a while. Tango was in Otillo, and Tango would put them up.

But luck—it could change. He had thought once to merely sell the girl, but now he wanted revenge. He wanted to silence her—for good.

He was not used to losing.

Hatfield was not a large town, and chances were, Pug thought, the girl was living in the hotel. There was only one.

He sent Bob in to snoop around and listen. Bob had a nondescript face and looked like any ordinary picker or drifter; there was no poster out with his picture on it—he'd never had a picture taken. He could go anywhere without question. But Pug warned him not to ask too many questions.

"Act a little dumb—that`s the best way. Then folks will explain things to you. Don't catch on too quick and they'll tell you more."

Bob nodded and rode into town, doing his best to look like a man with maybe sixbits in his pocket and a pig to sell. There was a saloon next to the hotel, and he got down in front of it and went inside, brushing off trail dirt. He had a story ready, in case anyone asked: He'd just come from the next town, Carson.

But nobody asked him.

And he didn't have to ask a single question. Three loud-mouths at the bar were gabbing about the blond beauty who was staying in the hotel. They had gaped, seeing her

45

tits bounce as she came down the stairs, and they were debating their chances of living the same exciting minutes once more.

Bob had a beer, looked in at the hotel, and got out. He rode back the way he'd come and reported to Pug that yes, the girl was in the hotel, according to saloon gossip, which was probably accurate.

Pug asked, "Did you see her yourself?"

"No. I listened to some peelers talking about her. They seen her yesterday. She's there all right. You got a plan?"

"I'm considerin' one."

But Bob had seen one more thing. "Your pitcher is up ever'where," he told Pug. "Somebody got hold of a photygraft and they got it on the dodgers."

Pug frowned. "Does it look like me?"

"Yeah, it does."

Pug rubbed his chin. "I ain't wearin' a beard. Only pitcher I had took, I was wearin' a beard."

"This one ain't got no beard."

"You're sure it was me?"

Bob nodded. "It's you, for a fact. It says they willing to pay one thousand for you."

"Is that all?"

"Well, I think you got to rob trains afore they raises the ante."

"Did you go into the hotel?"

Bob nodded again. "I put my head in. There's a desk and stairs to the right and a center hall all the way to the back, with doors on each side. I 'spect that's the same on the second floor. I didn't want to ask which room the girl is in."

"Is she alone?"

"I dunno, but I doubt it. Woman like her, she'd have friends, huh? Maybe that Chinaman is around somewhere—

maybe does her laundry. What's your plan?"

Pug scowled. "It depends on us locatin' her. We got to know where she is."

"I dunno how you going to find that out. Nobody's goin' to tell us, and we can't hang around the hotel."

That was true. Things weren't as easy as he'd thought they would be.

Marshal Leon Hacker had several friends he could count on, he said. They met in Ki's hotel room to discuss Pug Bennett and his gang. The friends were Andy Baile and two brothers, Walt and Hank Phelps, all three lean and capable-looking men.

If they could round up the Bennett gang, Ki told them, they would share in the considerable rewards. Pug was worth a thousand, Tipo and Bob about five hundred each, and they had a picture of Pug.

He would ask no part of the rewards, Ki promised. They would share it all between them.

He explained that Jessie had seen Pug shoot the banker, Mr. Oddum, and Pug was eager to eliminate her as a witness.

"Leon and I think Pug and the others are camping somewhere near town, hoping to bushwhack her if she shows herself."

"When d'you want to start looking?" Andy asked.

"Right away," Hacker said. He spread out a map of the vicinity. He had already marked likely hiding places. "They could be here, or here, or here. Maybe if we slide up easy we can surprise 'em. It's worth a try."

Everyone agreed. Two thousand dollars was a lot of incentive. And they might earn it quickly.

"But nobody takes chances," Hacker said firmly. "Shoot at the first wrong move. These three're worth just as much dead. And dead they a hell of a lot easier to handle . . . and save us money for a trial."

The first place they looked was an ancient limestone cave overhanging a creek several miles south of town. It was an ideal camping place: dry sandy floor and plenty of firewood handy. Hacker said he'd used it himself several times when caught in a summer rain. There was plenty of room under the shelf for horses.

Walt and Hank knew the place too, they said, and agreed it would make a fine hideout. Hacker led them to within a half mile of it, and they went the rest of the way through pine woods on foot—to find the cave empty and obviously unused.

Hacker's second choice was a deserted house and barn some five miles west of town. The house was tumbling down, the roof mostly gone, dangerous to enter. But the barn was still intact. No one had lived on the property for many years, and, Hacker said, no one knew who owned it, if anyone did. The barn would provide shelter for men and animals.

The house stood on a slight rise of ground with open fields around it and the barn. Ki used binoculars for an hour but could see no activity, and finally they approached.

No one had been in the barn for a very long time.

By then it was late afternoon; they returned to town for the night.

Ki found Jessica very unhappy, staying locked up in the hotel. "Tomorrow," she said, "I'm going with you."

Ki had expected this and had a ready answer. "Will you wear a man's coat and hat as a disguise?"

"If I must . . ."

"There's no sense in being more of a target than necessary."

"I suppose not. Very well, I agree."

48

The others were pleasantly surprised to see her when she saddled her horse in the morning. There were no objections to her riding with them. She put her blond locks up under the floppy hat, and with the coat pulled closed, no one would detect her presence, Ki was sure. Not unless he came near.

That morning Hacker led them north from the town instead of south. They rode for several hours till they came into a hilly region. He halted in a dense wood and spoke softly.

"They could be in this area. It's not very extensive. We ought to spread out and go in easy—look for camp-fire smoke."

Ki stayed close to Jessica for the first little while and was considering getting down to go forward on foot when Hank Phelps signaled excitedly with his arms, pointing. Hank was about a quarter of a mile to their left, and Ki studied the sky where he had indicated.

Was there a thin column of smoke rising? It was hard to detect in the high sky. He pointed it out to Jessie, and she nodded.

They joined Hank under a grouping of lush trees. His brother and Hacker were still farther to the left, he said. "I dunno if they seen it or not."

"Let's check," Ki suggested.

They slid down and left the horses, heading along the side of the hill, stepping in each other's tracks. There was little underbrush, for which they were grateful, and many deer trails. Ki worried that they would flush a deer that would run through the outlaws' camp.

As they rounded the hill, Hank, in the lead, motioned for them to halt. He got down and lay flat, and the others quickly did the same. Ahead of them, perhaps a hundred yards distant, was a shebang, a shelter built of branches and leaves. It was in a copse of trees, and beyond it three horses cropped grass.

Hank grinned over his shoulder.

Ki whispered, "Let's go back for the others."

Chapter 8

It took half an hour to silently round up the others and lead them back to the shebang. They were on its back side, and when they arrived, the horses were gone.

Ki swore and crept to the shelter. There was a smoldering fire in front of it. Someone had kicked dirt on the embers, but they still gave off a filmy column of smoke.

Ki moved around the shebang into the clear to look for tracks, and a sudden rifle shot came seeking him. He ducked, and a second shot hit the shelter, knocking it askew. The rifleman was on a horse two hundred yards away, at the edge of the trees. Hacker fired at him, and he spurred the horse and disappeared into the woods.

Hank yelled, "They headin' east!"

They had to go back for the horses, then gallop after the outlaws, who left an easy trail. The chase lasted for an hour and they got no closer. Then they came to a high rocky outcropping, with the trail threading into it.

Hacker halted out of rifleshot. "It's a perfect place for an ambush. We'll have to work around it."

Looking at the jumbled rocks, Ki sighed. To work around it would easily take an hour—or more. But if they continued on the trail, they might meet a deadly fire from three hidden guns. A terrible choice.

But Hacker was right; they had to go around, and try to pick up the trail again. They all grumbled, and it did take more than an hour to find a way around and get back to the outlaws' tracks.

Pug had sent Bob into Hatfield again to look and listen. He spent a long time sitting in a tilted-back chair across the street from the hotel, hoping to catch sight of the blond woman. But she did not appear.

After that he spent hours in several saloons, listening to the gab. He learned that Marshal Hacker was getting a posse together to flush out the gunmen who had robbed the bank and killed two people. The outlaws were thought to be in the vicinity.

When he heard that, Bob slid out. He hurried back to the shebang to warn Pug and Tipo. An unknown number of citizens would be searching for them very soon.

He had learned nothing about the girl. He could not even be sure she was still in Hatfield.

Pug hated to give up, but he was not stupid. It was obvious the girl was being protected, and she might have been moved to another town. He had not realized that it would be so difficult to get to her. She was becoming a symbol of bad luck in his mind, and it made him edgy.

He had a secret fear that he'd shared with no one, not even his wife. It had remained, brooding, in the depths of his thoughts for years. He'd tried to forget it—to bury it—but it always surfaced when danger arrived. It was a fear

destination; Ki and Jessie did not catch sight of them, not even with binoculars.

They lost the trail several times and had to spread out half a mile apart, looking for sign, which sometimes took hours. But when they came off the plains onto sagebrush flats, the tracks were plain; no attempt had been made to hide them. The outlaws, so far from Hatfield, obviously thought themselves in the clear.

They had no trouble following the tracks into Otillo.

It was mostly a shanty-lined street in a ramshackle town, and smelled to high heaven, especially downwind. The livery was in the center of town, with its sign printed in axle grease across the clapboard front. A smaller sign read: 25¢ PER DAY EA. HORSE.

There were five saloons along the wide, dusty street, a blacksmith shop and a freight yard at the end of town with corrals and sheds. Across from the livery was a rickety building that proclaimed itself the Palace Hotel with Snake Proof rooms.

It had eleven tiny cubicles that it called rooms. A clerk sat behind a raised table and wrote their names in a ledger. No, he had not seen three strangers come into town.

"You got rooms six and nine upstairs. Stable and privies out back. How long you fixin' to stay?"

"We're not sure," Ki said. "Maybe a week."

The clerk squinted at him. "You a Chinaman?"

"No. Half-Japanese. Is there a telegraph in town?"

"Telegraph! Jesus. Nearest one's a good hunnerd miles east at Fort Tillson. There's a trail goes thataway. You want one room'r two?"

"Two," Jessie said. "Is there another hotel in town?"

"No, only a few boardinghouses, and some at the freight yard. That'll be fifty cents f'each room."

Ki paid him. "Is there any law here?"

55

"We got us a marshal. Keeps the peace mostly. You ain't a lawman, I hope."

"No, I'm not. Why?"

The clerk grinned. "Folks run the last one outa town."

Otillo wasn't much as a town. Pug hadn't seen it for maybe five years, and it looked worse for the time, being more weather-beaten. But it was just as wild. Drunks fired at the moon every night, when there was a moon, and stars when there was not. There were only three things to do— drink, gamble or dally with the painted girls. Most visitors did all three.

A long time ago, the town had started as a couple of shacks at a crossroads, where wagons halted, where hide hunters, called stinkies, along with other downwind drifters, exchanged gossip and lies and drank sour mash out of tin cups.

Then other buildings took the place of tents, and pretty soon it was a town, but with no more law than the piney hill scrabblers had—which was not very damn much. Of course that fact attracted the loose element, and those folks a jump ahead of a posse, along with girls from the riverboats, who now worked the dance hall and the cribs along Front Street.

Otillo had only one saloon–dance hall, and it was owned and run by Tango. He had no other name, that anyone knew about. He was a tall man with black shiny hair and a narrow face with high cheekbones. Some said he had Indian blood. He was always smiling, always very well dressed in broadcloth pantaloons and usually a black frock coat and flowered vest. He was rattler quick with his sleeve derringers.

He practiced with the two guns every day, but he never sat in on table games any longer. Now he moved about the saloon, his black eyes darting here and there, seeing that everything was properly done, that the girls were busy, and his housemen on the job. No one crossed Tango.

And he seemed to know to a dollar what his take would be each night, just from judging the crowd. No one cheated Tango.

He and Pug Bennett went back a long way. They had first met when both were teens in Louisiana, when Pug was breaking into grocery stores and Tango was learning to deal faro.

Tango had put down roots in Otillo only because it was beyond the law. He promised himself that one day, when his pile was large enough, he would sell out and retire. He would buy himself a grand house with a river view and live the life of a gentleman—or the life he thought a gentleman should live.

Several times he had reached the limit he'd set himself, but had found it impossible to withdraw so early. He would miss the excitement and power his little empire gave him.

When Pug appeared suddenly one day, it was time for a celebration! Tango had a three-room apartment over the dance hall. He had supper and drinks brought up, and he and Pug dined and talked, bringing themselves up to date. Then the girls arrived.

Pug and Tango pulled the girls' clothes off and chased them about the rooms as the girls pretended to scream—not too loudly—and let themselves be caught . . . and a delightful time was had by all. It lasted most of the night, and they all slept till early afternoon of the next day.

Pug declared it the most fun he'd had since the Cat's Paw Club in New Orleans, years ago.

Tango found the three a room upstairs over the saloon. It had a bunk and he had two cots brought in. Pug and his friends would be his guests for as long as they cared to stay.

Tipo was especially happy with the accommodations because they were next to the whores' rooms along the upper hall. He set himself the task of learning all their names, as he frolicked with each and examined her for tattoos. Most of them had butterflies or some such in odd places. In the first week he tried out every girl, stripping each one naked and pounding his tool into its lair.

Each floozie was different, from barely interested to eager, from lethargic to enthusiastic. He settled on a girl named Cora. She had a man's penis tattooed on her round bottom; she was darkly blond and tawny and a little younger than the others—she said. She was glad to find a regular customer, and Tipo even bathed twice a week, just for her.

In the late afternoons, Pug frequently spent an hour or so with Tango. They often had supper together before Tango went into the saloon. Over the years, Tango had cultivated a number of hardcases—always for gain. People sold him information concerning the surrounding territories, from Kansas to Texas, even as far west as New Mexico Territory. He very frequently supplied money and equipment, even men, to owlhoots with good plans. Tango took a cut of the profits.

An experienced holdup man might come to him with a plan for robbing a bank, say in Arkansas. If he had the plan drawn on paper, and a map of the town with his getaway routes marked, and information about the bank, Tango might supply accomplices and grub money. For fifty percent.

Sometimes he lost, but usually he won. And the winnings far outstripped the losses. And when he lost, it was only money. The gunmen who entered the bank might come out feet-first and be accorded a county plot, soon forgotten, in the corner of the local boot hill, without a headboard.

Tango added to his retirement fund in this manner, and even though lawmen were aware of his activities, none could touch him in the Neutral Strip that some called No Man's Land.

Pug and Tango talked about these matters at length. Pug still had money in his sock from the Hatfield bank job, and did not need a grubstake, but he could always use good information. Tango had it.

There was a bank in Tannerville, Tango told him, just over the line in Missouri. It had not been even attempted in years. He had plans of it, fairly recent, and a good deal of information about the town itself, with getaway routes.

"It's just sitting there waiting for someone like you, Pug."

"You got recent plans, huh?"

"Yes. The gent who made them unfortunately got himself dead down in Texas before he could organize the job. No one but the two of us knew about the plans. Now you know."

"What's your cut?"

"Because it's you—fifteen percent. I usually get fifty when I have plans and money."

"Can three of us do the job?"

Tango nodded. "I think so. Four might be better, so one man could hold the horses. I had a case last year where no one was with the horses and some citizen stampeded them and my friends were trapped in the bank. Very bad. I can find you a fourth man if you want."

Pug made a face. "I hate t'split four ways. Lemme think about it."

"Sure. But don't wait too long. Things change. The plan might not be any good in a few months or someone'll get there ahead of you." Tango smiled. "But I don't need to tell you that."

Pug discussed the idea with Bob. Tipo as usual was on a mattress with Cora. Bob was in favor of the job. He liked the idea of going to Missouri, then coming back to Otillo. "If we play our cards right they'll never think of lookin' for us here."

"It's a long damn trip, probably three hunnerd miles each way."

"Yeah, but that's in our favor. They'll look closer to home for whoever did it, won't they?"

Pug shrugged. "Maybe so . . ." He sighed. "You figger we can pry Tipo offen that blonde long enough to talk to him about what we gonna do?"

Bob nodded. "It'll come outa her like a cow's leg outa the mud." He made a sound with his lips, and they both laughed.

★
Chapter 9

The tracks of the three outlaws had led into Otillo, but did the three men go on through, or did they stop? They had not taken rooms in the hotel. But of course there were many other places they could be.

Ki sidled into the largest saloon, the Wild Horse. It was also a dance hall; a sign said the band started playing at 6 P.M. In the meantime a piano player at the far end of the saloon kept music alive, entertaining perhaps twenty men and half a dozen painted doves. Many of the customers were sitting at tables, gabbing or playing cards. The girls wandered from one table to the next . . .

Ki ordered a beer at the bar and sipped it, looking the place over. It was not new; it had been there for some time. The long bar was polished on top and terribly scarred below. The back bar had obviously been replaced many times. Ki noted a few bullet holes there and dozens in the ceiling. Only a few of the hanging lamps were lighted, but the rest would be soon. The dance hall was empty and dark. He could see a stage at one end, so evidently they had shows of one kind or another.

He did not see Pug Bennett.

Before dark he returned to the hotel and talked to Jessie. It was possible that Bennett was not in the town.

They went to the restaurant for supper.

Bob was in the restaurant when the blond girl and her Chinaman companion entered and took a table. They did not know his face, and he finished his steak and coffee and slid out to report to Pug that they'd been followed.

Pug was annoyed that they had been tailed, but pleased to hear the girl was in town. She was making it easy for him.

"I want you 'n' Tipo to put her on a horse and take 'er out in the sticks. A long way out. Let the buzzards have her."

"All right. What about the Chinaman?"

"Kick his ass outa the way. I don't care about him. I'll ask Tango for the borrow of a horse."

Bob nodded. "You want we should do it tonight?"

"Why not? The sooner the better. Get some rope to tie her up with. I'll talk to Tango and meet you in the stable in an hour."

"All right." Bob went to find Tipo. He found the other half-asleep in bed with a naked girl. He got up grumpily and pulled on his clothes.

Bob went down to the stable and got some heavy twine from the stableboy, then saddled the horses. When Pug came in and pointed to a sorrel, he slapped a saddle on. Tipo showed up, yawning, but he got more interested when Pug told him what they were about. The blond girl would provide them some entertainment before she joined her ancestors.

They walked down the alley to the hotel and tied the horses by the rear door. Bob went in to find out from the clerk which room the girl occupied.

"She's in nine," the clerk said.

"Is she in the room?"

The clerk shrugged. "I dunno. I seen her go out a while back. I dunno if she come in again."

Bob went out to tell Pug the girl might be in her room and might not be. "What you want to do?"

Pug was exasperated. He told Tipo, "You stay with the horses." To Bob he said, "Let's go up and see." He climbed the stairs. On the second floor he drew his pistol and held it down by his side. Bob did the same.

At the door of number 9, Bob rapped heavily.

There was no answer.

Bob rapped again and kicked the door. "She ain't in," he said and looked around at Pug.

A door opened across the hall, several doors down, and the girl looked into the hall. "What is it?"

Pug showed her his pistol. "C'mere, girl—"

Then he frowned as the Chinaman pulled the girl inside and said, "What is it you want?" His hand was holding onto his vest.

Bob stepped forward and cocked his pistol, leveling it at the slim, black-haired man. "We want the girl."

Pug saw the Chinaman move; then he was conscious of a flash of light. Bob's revolver fired into the ceiling, and he stumbled, reeling against the wall, clutching at his throat. Pug stared at him in astonishment, seeing his hands turn red with blood. Bob's gun clattered away and he sprawled on the floor.

Pug fired and kept firing—as he ran toward the back stairs. He emptied the pistol, jumped down the steps three at a time, and yelled at Tipo. They both dashed away on the horses. What the hell had killed Bob? It was like the Chinaman had thrown a bolt of lightning! It had torn out Bob's throat!

At Tango's stable they got down and went upstairs. Pug felt curiously cold; his hands were still shaking. It might have been him instead of Bob, but Bob had threatened the Chinaman. What kind of magic did the man have?

Now there was only himself and Tipo.

He wanted a drink bad. Tipo was asking questions. What had happened up there? Did Bob get shot? Pug told him disjointedly and sent him down to the saloon for a bottle.

Jesus! Was he really losing his nerve?

Ki had thrown the *shuriken* and pulled back into the room as Pug fired and kept firing.

Jessie said, "That was Pug Bennett!"

"Yes, it was."

Ki waited till the firing stopped and then looked into the hall. Pug had gone and the other man was dead, crumpled by the wall. He retrieved the throwing star and wiped it on the downed man's shirt. He wouldn't care.

The clerk from downstairs yelled up, "Who's shooting?"

Jessie went to the steps and told him, "It's all over." He came up to stare at the body. A few roomers came out to look and ask questions.

Ki took the clerk aside. "He tried to shoot Miss Starbuck. Better get somebody to remove the body. Is there an undertaker in town?"

"Yeah, I'll get him," the clerk said and disappeared.

Ki took Jessie inside and closed the door. "That's certainly one of Pug Bennett's men. So now he only has one other besides himself." He smiled at her. "We're whittling them down."

"Won't he enlist more?"

"I expect so. But our fight is with him and the one they call Tipo. The enlistees may not want to fight another's battles." He looked at her. "You want to stay in town?"

"I want to see Pug Bennett tried for murder."

Ki smiled. "That answers that."

"They know we're here, and they probably know why . . ."

"So they'll try to eliminate us—as they just did try." Ki heard noises from the hall and opened the door. Three men were hauling the body downstairs.

He wondered if the marshal would come calling.

★

Chapter 10

The fact that Bob had been killed in the hotel—by curious and unknown means—was the talk of the saloons. Pug explained to Tango that he had seen only a flash.

"Something hit Bob—I dunno what! But it come fast as lightning! Hit him in the throat."

"You never saw what it was?"

"Hell, I was scared another flash would be coming! I shot at the goddam Chinaman and kept shootin' till I got out of there!"

The undertaker, Mr. Briscoe, said the victim's throat had been torn out by some very sharp tool or object. Bob had died almost instantly. Tango was very interested in this development.

He asked Briscoe, "The thing that caused the death was not on the body when you received it?"

"No, sir. Nothing was. Whatever it was killed him had been took away."

Pug growled, "The goddam Chinaman took it."

Tango said, "Was it like a knife?"

Briscoe pursed his lips. "Yes—and no. It was something razor sharp all right, but not like a blade." He made a helpless gesture. "That's my opinion, sir. Maybe I'm wrong, but a knife thrown that distance wouldn't make that wound. I seen a lot of knife wounds in my time. Mr. Pug said the man was standin' maybe fifteen feet away."

Pug nodded.

"Then it was something else," Tango said slowly. "I'd sure as hell like to know what." He let Briscoe go and looked at Pug. "You say the thing was silent?"

"Never made a sound. All I know, I seen a kind of silvery flash—then it hit Bob and he made some choking sounds and fell down."

"Where does this Chinaman come from?"

"Hell, I dunno. Afore this, I never thought he amounted to much."

"Apparently he does . . ."

Pug said, "You don't think it's some kind of magic, do you?"

Tango made a face. "I don't believe in magic. He threw something at Bob, that's all."

Pug grunted. "I need somebody who's good with a rifle."

"I can supply that." Tango smiled. "I've got a kid who's an expert. I'll send someone for him."

"After what happened," Ki said, "this hotel is not very secure. Too many people are in and out every day. We'd best make a change."

"What do you suggest? There's no other hotel . . ."

Ki had a slip of paper. "I found this tacked up on the livery stable wall along with some other notices." He handed it over.

Jessie looked at it, then at him. "Rooms for rent? It says

67

'apply at freight yard.' " Her brows went up.

"I went there. They've got five rooms—pretty small ones. The yard was once a way station, till the stageline discontinued the route."

"Why, do you think they'll be any better than here?"

"Well, for one thing, less foot traffic. There's only one way in or out, and the freight office windows overlook each room."

"Then let's move."

Ki sent a boy to the freight office with a deposit and a request for two rooms. That evening, long after dark, they made the move, staying off the main street.

When they were settled in, Jessie said, "The odds here are stacked against us, aren't they? We're in a town where the U.S. Marshal can't help—he isn't even allowed here. Do you think we have a chance of arresting Pug Bennett and taking him to the nearest law?"

"Not much chance," Ki admitted. "We're targets ourselves. Bennett obviously has friends here. They may not help him against us, but they'll hide him."

"If they do that, it's a standoff, isn't it?"

"I'm afraid so. Do you want to go back to Hatfield?"

Jessie shrugged dejectedly. "No, I don't want to . . . but I wonder if we're not on a wild goose chase. We're getting nowhere fast."

The "kid" that Tango had mentioned turned out to be a cold-faced young man with a pronounced limp. His name was J. L. Deacon. He told them, "Most folks calls me Deak." He had a scrolled Winchester with him.

Pug explained about the girl and the Chinaman and offered two hundred dollars for each of them, payment to be made when one or both was draining on the undertaker's slab, awaiting burial.

This was acceptable to Deak. There weren't many Chinamen around and the blond girl was one of the few females in town not a cyprian, working the saloons. He should have no trouble centering them.

Privately he thought it is a terrible waste, killing a woman, but two hundred was two hundred. That kind of money didn't come along every day. And of course there *were* lots of women around . . .

The two were staying at the Palace Hotel, on the second floor. That was where Bob had been killed. Pug told Deak the Chinaman had thrown a knife into Bob's throat.

Deak went to the hotel to mosey through it, limping up the stairs. The ugly bloodstain was still on the floor. Deak stared at it. He didn't like the idea of a knife thrower. Pug had said, "Don't let him come too close . . ."

He had no intention of it. He took up a station across the street from the hotel, next to the livery. There was an old shack there that faced away from the street but had a small window through which he could see the front door of the hotel. He paced off the distance as he crossed the street. It was an easy shot, and an easy route away. He could go past the livery corrals, and probably no one would see him at all.

He spent the entire day in the shack, and neither the girl nor her Chinaman companion appeared. Was Pug's information good? Deak should have checked it before wasting the day. He went across and asked the clerk about the two.

"They moved out," the clerk said. "Day'r two ago."

"Shit! Where did they go?"

"They didn' say."

Deak went back to see Tango. "Them two'r not in the hotel."

"They're not?"

"The clerk don't know where they went."

Tango was not acting. "Damn!"

"Where's Pug? Maybe he knows something else."

Tango sighed. "He's on his way to Missouri. He won't be back for weeks."

"Ummm." Deak stared at Tango's diamond stickpin. "Then what you want me to do?"

"Stick around." Tango rubbed his chin. "I'll put out the word and we'll see what turns up."

★

Chapter 11

Jessie quickly made friends with the woman in the freight office. She was the bookkeeper and the owner's wife. Her name was Leona, and she had just arrived in town that week to discover that she was one of very few wives in the entire Strip—or so she had been told. She was delighted to see Jessica, and they had coffee together each morning.

Leona was very interested to learn that Jessica and Ki were after the man who had killed their banker friend in Hatfield. Leona's husband had once been a lawman, before he got into freighting. That was a secret, of course. The shady element in Otillo might not appreciate it and could take certain steps.

She had heard of Pug Bennett, Leona said, but had never seen him. Being in her husband's office, she heard many things from the drivers and hostlers; often she listened when they did not know it.

In this manner she heard about Deak. He was generally disliked and considered to be one who was always cocked and ready to fire. He had a reputation as a killer, and the main reason he stayed in the Strip was that there the law could not get at him.

He had been seen talking to Tango very recently, and that boded ill for somebody as a rule.

Leona mentioned it to Jessie. "The man is an assassin."

Ki was on his guard. He watched a man with a limp come into the area of the freight-yard rooms to look it over. Leona saw him through the office window. It was Deak all right, she told Ki.

It was no trick for Ki to follow him. Deak entered one of several ramshackle buildings across from the freight yard. Then he came out and entered Tango's saloon.

In her room, Jessie said, "If Leona is right, he's very dangerous."

Ki nodded. "And if he's after us, he'll try to pick us off from across the street."

"Then we should leave."

"Let's make sure . . . Later on I'll go over there and wait for him. Let's see what he does."

What Deak did was station himself with a rifle and wait, watching the entrance to the freightyard rooms. Ki watched him until the light faded. The man *was* an assassin. When the light was gone, Ki followed him to the saloon and sat across the room as he talked to Tango.

The room was crowded; Ki took a chair by the wall. He was certain that Tango had never seen him, but he kept his hat brim down. Pug Bennett was not in the room.

It occurred to him then to ask the stable boy. The lad was half-asleep on a cot. Ki shook him awake, pressing a coin into the boy's hand. "I'm looking for Pug. Have you seen him?"

"Pug?" The lad yawned. "Oh, you mean Mr. Bennett?"

"Yes. What's happened to him?"

The lad looked at him curiously. "He went to Missouri."

Ki was astonished. "Missouri?"

"Yeah, some business there. Maybe Tango sent him. You oughta talk to Tango."

"Yes, I will. Is he coming back?"

The boy shrugged. "I dunno."

Ki thanked him and went back to talk to Jessie. "The stable boy tells me Pug went to Missouri."

She was just as surprised. "That's a very long ride! Why did he go?"

"The boy didn't know. It can't be for a humanitarian or legal reason. Maybe it's to commit a crime."

"Probably." She looked at him glumly. "How long will he be gone . . . weeks, I suppose."

"I expect so."

"Then there's no point in our staying here, is there?"

Ki thought of the rifleman. "No. Let's pack up. I vote we leave tonight."

She nodded. "I'll write a note to Leona."

After midnight on a Monday the town was dark and silent; even the saloons were closed. Ki made certain no one was waiting for them on the street.

They were miles from the town at sunup.

Leon Hacker was surprised and delighted to see them when they rode into town. But he was sorry they had not been able to hog-tie Pug Bennett and drag him back for trial.

He was glad to hear that only one other member of the gang, Tipo, still survived, and used Ki's exact words: "You're whittling them down."

73

They had been in Hatfield about two weeks when the newspaper came out with this headline: Bank Robbed In Tannerville, Mo. The story detailed how Pug Bennett and his gang had walked in and filled their sacks with greenbacks. Bennett himself had been recognized by half a dozen witnesses who had seen the posters. The gang had gotten away with about fifteen thousand dollars.

Ki said, "That's why he went to Missouri."

"And that's why we'll go there," Jessie replied.

The Tannerville Bank had turned out to be all that Tango had said it would be. He had supplied them well, with a street map showing three different routes out of town and a plan of the bank's interior and the two guards' stations.

When they looked it over, they saw that the layout was exactly as stated. Tango's information was precise and up-to-date.

The getaway route they selected went across the town from the bank, into a field, and through it to some low hills. Beyond the hills they had a choice of roads.

The two guards in the bank were elderly men, potbellied and gray, but probably ex-policemen. Tango had advised caution with them.

With Bob gone, Pug knew that he and Tipo could not do the job properly, so Tango had been asked to supply another man. He sent them Jonas Olcott, known as Jonesy, a lanky, loose-jointed man with an easy disposition but experience at six-gun withdrawals.

They had left Otillo three days before Deak was hired to do away with the girl and the Chinaman.

It had been taken them a week and a half to arrive at the outskirts of Tannerville; they timed it to get there at night and found it a town about three times the size of Otillo and much better kept up.

The bank was on a corner of the main street and a side street that petered out before it reached the hills. The building was of red brick and had gold leaf on the windows and a black iron awning over the wide front doors. The second story seemed deserted.

Many of the other buildings on the street looked like mail-order affairs, bought from a catalog and shipped west, not an unusual thing.

Pug and Tipo went into the bank to change money and examined the town carefully. The marshal's office was a block away, on another side street. The bank guards were old and half-asleep in the late afternoon, just before closing time.

"Let's not wait around," Pug said. "We'll go in just before they close up."

It was smooth. Tipo and Jonesy disarmed the guards, shoved them, the bank officers, and the customers into a room, and locked the door. Then they filled the sacks they'd brought along, went out, and rode off along the side street.

"Nothing to it," Pug said. "No trouble, no fuss."

As they crossed the fields and reached the low hills, they could hear the alarm bell ringing.

If there was a pursuit, they did not see it. Pug said, "They're all disorganized to hell. Probably never get together."

They rode steadily, crossed several creeks and forested areas, and did not stop to sleep for two days. Then they found a dense woods and laid up for a full day, sleeping and eating.

After that they counted the money.

Tango had said he'd only take fifteen percent, instead of his usual fifty, so Pug counted it and put it aside and divided the rest, which came to nearly four thousand each. It made a big bulge in each man's pocket.

When they started out again the next morning, they were lost. They followed no road but headed, they were sure, generally west, into the setting sun. The land was vast and empty; they met no one.

A day later they found a boatman on a creek; he was fishing and told them they were thirty miles from Hollings, which was due west. With that knowledge under their hats, they began to talk easy, about spending money and about horses. Tipo talked about women until they shut him up.

Then they came to a ridge and, halting to get an idea of the lay of the land, saw building shapes in the misty distance. It was Hollings, a town catering mostly to ranchers and a few small farmers. It had nine saloons, three dance halls, and one small, ramshackle church at the end of town, like an afterthought.

As they rode in, several floozies came to the open windows above one of the saloons and yelled and whistled at them. One shouted, "A dollar a throw . . ."

Tipo yelled and waved his hat. "Now we talkin' turkey," he said happily.

Hollings proved to be a wide-open town. A liveryman told them, "You gets drunk and bawls at the moon or falls offen a wagon, the marshal'll lock you up for a day'r two till you sobers, that's all. We have a little shootin' but Doc Maddie takes care o'that."

"He the town doc?"

"No. He's the undertaker."

Jonesy had never owned so much money before in his life. His shady activities in the past had brought him at times hundreds of dollars. Now he had thousands!

The first night in town he got very drunk and bought the house a round—which disgusted Pug. It brought attention to him. And subsequently he and Tipo had to carry the helpless

Jonesy into his room at the hotel and dump him on the bed, snoring.

Pug flung Jonesy's hat into a corner. "The sombitch is a drunk! I bet you he drinks up his cut in a week—or gives it away." He glowered at the snoring man. "That goddam Tango shouldn't never have loaded us with a drunk."

"It's his money," Tipo observed, his mind on the little black-haired charmer he'd seen in the saloon.

Pug only grunted.

He worried that night, and the next morning he hunted up Tipo. "Get your possibles together. We hitting the trail in a hour."

"We leavin' town!?"

"Let's go." Pug looked over Tipo's shoulder. "You got a woman in here?"

"Maybe . . ."

"Git rid of her. We got to go. I'll meet you in the stable."

"Something happen?"

"Not yet, but we can't trust Jonesy. Sooner or later he's going to shoot his mouth off while he's drunk. Drunks is the worst thing in creation. Hurry up. Git rid of that gal. This here party is over."

Tipo sighed. Well, her tits were pretty small anyhow.

★
Chapter 12

When he struggled out of bed the next afternoon—with a terrible head—Jonesy could not find either Pug or Tipo. He gave it up after a short search; they were probably down in one of the saloons. He soaked some cold towels and lay down with them on his head.

That evening he felt a bit better, and he looked in the stable. Pug's horse and Tipo's were both gone. And the clerk told him they had left the hotel.

He realized then that they had gone on without him.

Well, damn them—he didn't need them! He went into the nearest saloon and bought a bottle. When he sat down with it, Fanny showed up. She was a bar girl.

She massaged his thigh under the stable. "Le's go upstairs, honey." She was dark and her dress was low cut and her hand was bold as hell.

He was three drinks ahead of her. "M'partners gone and lef' me, Fanny."

"You got partners?"

"I did—for the job. But they gone on wi'out me."

"What job?"

"Huh?" He looked at her blearily.

"What job was that?"

"Job we did in T-Tannerville."

Fanny leaned in close, her hand cupping him, and he smelled her heavy perfume. She said, "Izzat where you got all the money—the bank in Tannerville?"

Jonesy grinned. "I didn't say that. Le's go."

"What?"

"Le's go upstairs, like you said."

"Yeah, all right. Can you walk?"

He pushed her away. "Course I can. You figger I'm drunk!" He grabbed the bottle and clumped up the stairs, humming a song he'd heard somewhere.

In her cubicle, she poured out drinks and let him paw her, half undress her, as he sopped up the whiskey. Finally she pushed him down and sat on his chest and waited till he began to snore.

Then she went through his pockets and found the wad of money, amazed at so much! He had spent a lot, but there were still thousands here! Jesus Christ! It made her head swim. What should she do? She took half of it and shoved it into her reticule. Benny, her "employer," knew Jonesy had money—she'd give him some. She hurried downstairs and got Benny aside, showing him the roll.

He grabbed it. "Where'd you git this?"

"Customer. He's up in my room now."

Benny riffled through the bills. "Is this all of it?"

"Of course. Gimme that back . . ."

"You workin' in my house. You git a third. He's sleepin' it off up there?"

"Yeah."

"Who is he?"

"I think he robbed the bank in Tannerville."

"The paper said there was three of 'em."

"He said he had partners."

Benny frowned. "Where are they?"

"I dunno."

He counted out the money into her hand. "Here's yours. You git back to work. I'll get the boys to take care of him. If his partners come in, you don't know shit."

She nodded. When he left, she put the third into the reticule with the rest of the money and smiled to herself.

The bank manager in Tannerville said, "No one was hurt in the robbery. Everyone complied at once to the demands. They locked us up in a room, but I had a key, and when we heard them leave, I unlocked the door."

Jessie said, "You were luckier than some."

There had been three robbers, and one was certainly Pug Bennett; he was short and red-haired. Another was probably the man called Tipo, Dominic Tipo, who was known to ride with Bennett.

The third man could not be identified and was likely someone Bennett had picked up for the job. A dozen people had seen the robbers leave the bank and head for the hills. The route was pointed out to Jessie and Ki, almost due west.

Jessie said, "They're probably going back to Otillo."

Ki agreed. "But they might stop and celebrate along the way. Let's have a look at the map."

The map showed three towns along the route west; the largest was Hollings. It was also the closest.

They reached it in two days.

The local law was a deputy sheriff, a large man with a big belly and florid face. He sat behind a desk eating an apple when they entered. He had seen nothing, heard nothing. "No bank robbers stopped off here, folks."

"How can you be so positive?" Jessie asked.

"Because I know m'town." The deputy pointed to his ears. "I hear things ever'day. Nothin' like that is goin' to git by me."

Jessie thanked him politely.

When they were alone, Ki said, "He's a fathead. I doubt if anyone tells him anything—that amounts to anything." He glanced at the sky. "I think I'll snoop around for a bit. Maybe I can hear something . . ."

"I'll be at the hotel."

Ki heard nothing at all in the saloons, but as he was passing the stage station, there was a ruckus in the yard just outside the waiting room door. Two men were pulling a girl off a stagecoach. Curious, he approached. The girl was swearing at them, screaming and kicking; she did not want to get off.

Several other passengers stood nearby, staring. The driver and his shotgun guard started to interfere, but the men warned them, saying something Ki could not hear.

But when one of the men cuffed the girl, slapping her down viciously, Ki was annoyed. He kicked the slapper in the butt, and both men turned to face him, astonished to see a relatively slight black-haired man.

The closest man charged Ki at once, and Ki's downward kick, a *gedan barai,* stopped him short. Before the other man could react, Ki slipped one hand under the downed man's elbow, keeping a grip on his wrist, exerted pressure, and cracked the bone like a dry twig. The man screamed and fell, clutching his arm.

The second man pulled a revolver, and Ki side-kicked him in the chest, spun around, and kicked his hip bone. The gun clattered away, and the man went down heavily.

Ki picked up the gun and slid it into his belt, waiting. The man got up slowly, eyeing him, seeming about ready to charge—then he thought better of it. He pulled his moaning companion up, and they left, muttering threats.

The girl was half-crying, half-swearing, one hand pressing a hankie to her cut cheek.

Ki said, "What was all that about?"

She got up painfully. "They wanted t'stop me from goin'."

"Why would they want that?"

She glanced at him and shook her head. "I dunno."

She was a terrible liar; he didn't believe it for a second. "You work in a saloon?" She was dressed like a whore.

She sniffed and nodded.

The driver said, "We fixin' to go—you goin' with us?"

The girl climbed into the stagecoach, and Ki shut the door. She put her head out the open window. "Thanks, mister."

Ki waved, and the coach rattled out to the street. He had been in town about an hour and managed to make two enemies. He sighed and hunted up the station manager, Mr. Taber.

Taber told him, "She worked at Benny's place, the Slipper. Name of Fanny. Those girls are always coming and going."

"Who were the two men?"

"They work for Benny. I've seen 'em both in there many a time."

"Why do you suppose they'd try to stop her?"

Taber shrugged. "Maybe she had something they wanted—that Benny wanted."

Ki went out to the street and stared after the departing stage. What would that be but money? Maybe Fanny had held out on Benny.

● ● ●

Benny Kubik was in a rage. Two of his bouncers had been knocked on their asses by a man half their size, and Biggs had a broken wrist. They told Benny the man was a Chinaman who had suddenly interfered and kept them from pulling Fanny off the stagecoach. She had left with it. And the money. He knew she had money.

He had tried to stop her because she had packed a bag in a hurry and run to the stage station. That meant she had held out—this had happened before to him. Whores were thieves. You had to watch them every minute.

Fanny had come downstairs with a wad of bills from the bank robber's pocket—that in itself was suspicious when he thought about it. Of course she'd done it because she wanted him to get rid of the man.

Whores were not the brightest people he'd ever met, and Fanny was definitely not a deep thinker. Probably seeing a big wad of money, thousands, had flustered her and she'd done everything wrong. Then she'd tried to run out. Benny wondered how much she'd gotten away with.

That damned Chinaman had cheated him out of all of it!

And then the Chinaman showed up in his saloon! Benny was astonished to see him put a revolver on the bar. "This belongs to one of your men."

The bartender nodded and put it on the backbar. "I'll see he gets it."

"A girl named Fanny worked here?"

"Sure, she does. Ever'body knows Fanny." He grinned. "Inside and out."

"Do you know why she left?"

The barman was surprised. "I didn't know she did."

"She was evidently with one customer most of the night—"

The barman shook his head. "Didn't see her or him." He walked away.

Benny heard the exchange and walked out the back, gritting his teeth. The damned Chinaman was asking too many questions. The bank robber from Fanny's room was pushing up the daisies out in the sticks. It would not do for the Chinaman to find out.

He went across the alley to Hamp's room. If anybody could settle the nosy man's hash it was Hamp, who was very quick with a gun. He would pop the Chink before he could get close.

Hamp wasn't in his room; he was in the stable, rubbing down a horse.

"Got a job f'you," Benny said.

"What kinda job?"

"Somebody needs to get dead."

Hamp smiled.

★

Chapter 13

Ki returned to the hotel, and he and Jessie sat in chairs in the fading light, outside on the walk, as he told her about the encounter at the stage station.

Jessie asked, "Why do you think she was running away?"

"Well, of course it could have been for a dozen reasons, but likely money. I talked to a bartender in the saloon where she worked, but he could not or would not tell me anything." He smiled. "What if it were Tipo?"

"Interesting."

"If Tipo let the wrong person know he was carrying a large sum of money?"

"Something might have happened to him . . . and the bartender isn't talking."

"It's a theory. But it raises a lot of questions, such as: If the girl got the money—how did she get it? Was she in it with someone else? How did Benny get into the picture? Things don't add up."

Jessie frowned. "We don't know all the facts."

"True. But one fact is—Pug Bennett is not in town or he'd be in the middle of all of this. Did he leave Tipo behind?"

"He might. That's not hard to believe."

"Yes. Then did Benny get rid of Tipo?"

Jessie nodded. "He could have—if he thought he was getting a large sum thereby."

"Then how did the girl get away with it? If she did?"

Jessie laughed. "All right, I give up. How did she?"

"A very good question. I should have asked her before I put her on the stage."

Jonesy had talked before he cashed in his chips, telling about Pug and Tipo and the robbery money they had divided up. A lot of money.

Benny Kubik enlisted Hamp in this—the Chinaman could wait—and set out after Pug and Tipo, who would have thousands in their war bags . . . and who did not know Benny or Hamp from Ginny's mule. Jonesy had also mentioned Otillo in the Strip, saying he and the others were heading there.

He and Hamp would be able to approach the two robbers with no trace of suspicion, and open up from three feet away. Easy money.

When they rode into Stebbins, Benny asked questions and was told that two gents had been through town five or six hours earlier, one short and red-haired.

They were on the right trail.

They swapped horses and hurried on—and caught up to the two in Ryesburg. Pug and Tipo were in the hotel. It was a small house with a tiny lobby area, barely large enough for two men to stand before the desk.

They started to question the young clerk, who then explained that he had just come on duty and had no idea if the two men they sought were in their rooms or not.

Then the clerk looked up and pointed. "Ask him. That's one of them."

Tipo heard the clerk and halted. He had never seen the two men before—but one of them went for his gun! Tipo stumbled back, pulling his own iron, firing too soon. A fusillade of shots battered the walls of the little room. Tipo was hit again and again, dropped his pistol, and crumpled on the steps.

The clerk was facedown on the floor behind the desk.

Benny went up the stairs and prodded Tipo. Dead. He quickly searched the body and pocketed a wad of bills. He heard voices along the hall as doors were opened. What had happened? What was all the shooting?

Benny reloaded, looking for Pug to show himself, but he did not. Maybe he was in one of the saloons.

He and Hamp went out to the street. One down, one more to go.

Pug was in the stable behind the hotel. When he heard the shooting, he slid into the hotel watchfully and up to the second floor, pistol in hand. Other roomers were crowding into the hall, chattering. He heard them say that someone had been shot down on the stairs.

Pushing through the gawkers, Pug looked down at Tipo's body. Tipo had been hit numerous times and was a bloody mess, very dead. Pug took a long breath and let it out.

"Who shot him?" he said to those around him on the stairs. No one answered.

The desk clerk was scared and rattled, very white-faced. He had never been so close to a shooting before, he said. Bullets were flying everywhere. A picture on the wall over the desk had been smashed.

Pug pressed him. Who had done the shooting?

"T-two men come in," the clerk stammered.

"What did they look like?"

The clerk could not describe either. They had pulled guns and started shooting, and he ducked down behind the desk, flat on the floor till it was over.

Pug shook him in annoyance. "Two *men* came in? Not a man and a woman?"

"No—it was two men. I never seen 'em before." The clerk fought free.

Pug went back to the stable before the law arrived to question everyone. Tipo was dead! He sat down and swore, shoulders hunched. First Windy, then Bob, and now Tipo. Was *he* next?

Two men were after him? Who could they be? Not the law or they'd have stayed around. Maybe bounty hunters hoping to collect on both of them. But how would ordinary bounty hunters know where they were? And how could he defend against shadows? He'd have to consider every man his enemy.

He saddled his horse and tied on the blanket roll, then rode along the alley to the next street. A grocery store was still open. He got down and bought vittles, put them in a grain sack, and tied it on.

It was full dark when he mounted the horse and rode slowly out of town, the pistol in his hand. Who the hell were the two men? If he went toward Otillo, would they follow? How much did they know? How had they found him?

Nothing but questions! Never a damned answer.

Hell, those two could turn up anywhere, start a conversation with him, and shoot him in the belly! He'd have to be very careful who got close to him.

Maybe he should stay clear of Otillo. He had lots of money—he even had Tango's share of the robbery. If he did not go to Otillo, then where?

He walked the horse along the road leading west and thought about it. There were plenty of towns . . . Where would the law look for him?

Not in Otillo. He snapped his fingers. Not in Puente either!

His wife lived in Puente. He hadn't seen her in several years—they had not parted friends. But she had always liked money; she was the saving type. He could pay her to hide him for a while.

He turned it over and over in his mind. Had he told anyone where she lived? He didn't remember mentioning it—why should he? No one talked about women to him. How could those strangers who had shot Tipo know about Frances, his wife?

The last he'd heard she had even changed back to her maiden name. They'd never find her. Or him.

According to the weekly, a man named Benny Kubik had claimed the five-hundred-dollar reward offered for Dominic Tipo. Kubik had witnesses and a paper signed by the local law that said he had shot Tipo in a hotel in Ryesburg.

Ki got out the map and found Ryesburg, pointing it out to Jessie. "It's generally on the route to Otillo."

Jessie read the item in the paper. "It doesn't mention Pug Bennett except to say that Tipo rode with him."

"The law could be keeping mum about Bennett so they don't alert him. Bennett was probably in Ryesburg with Tipo, so maybe the law knows where he went."

"Maybe. *We* think he's on the way to the Strip, but maybe not. He's stayed alive a long time by being unpredictable."

"That's true," Ki said, musing. "He's a very slippery customer." He looked at her. "Where would he go if he doesn't head for Otillo?"

Jessie shrugged her shapely shoulders lightly. "Anywhere! He could have a hideout all planned for the occasion. The question is—should *we* go to Otillo?"

"I'm afraid so. It *is* in the Strip and it means safety to him. He can thumb his nose at the law from there. That fact may override everything else."

She sighed. "I'll get my things together . . ."

It was summertime and hot on the plains. A few snarls of cloud were slowly unraveling on the far horizon. The sun beat down, and their shadows rippled among the sparse, bristling patches of brush. At night a burnt half moon hung in the east.

They avoided a dust storm one day and ran into another the next, watching for twisters. The distances shimmered, and their clothes were filmed with fine dust.

And then the town appeared, a few rooflines and columns of gray smoke, then solid buildings, weather-beaten and long-settled. The hotel gathered them in and provided baths and clean clothes.

But no one had seen Pug Bennett—or so they said.

Somehow Pug Bennett had avoided Benny and Hamp, even though Benny was sure he did not know their faces.

But it had not been a total waste of time. There was the reward. Also, Tipo had had almost three thousand dollars on him that Benny had pocketed . . . and not mentioned to Hamp. Hamp knew that the two outlaws had money, but he did not know how much, and he had not seen Benny pocket the roll. For one reason the tiny room had been filled with powder smoke.

Benny told him he hadn't had time to go through Tipo's pockets.

But for the company, he allowed Hamp free drinks in the saloon for a week.

• • •

Puente was the center of a farming community, a pretty little town well off the beaten track. No one went there except for business, buying or selling. The town had one saloon and no soiled doves or gambling.

If a man wanted a spree or a celebration, he went to Harding, twenty miles south. It had everything and never closed.

Puente, some said, could not be told from a cemetery; it was that quiet.

Frances Urshel was still married to Pug, though she now used her maiden name. She wanted no connection to him, however tenuous. She and Pug had parted because of his notoriety—and a few other things. Over the years a procession of lawmen had come rapping on her door, inquiring about him. None of them seemed to believe a thing she told them. They asked the same questions over and over again as if to trip her up.

She frequently saw his name in the paper; he was wanted for this or that. The reward offered for his arrest had steadily mounted from four hundred dollars to a thousand. Sometimes his name was coupled with that of a woman. Whenever she had confronted him with it, he denied any alliance, or said the woman was probably a plant of the law, trying to trap him.

At first it had been exciting to be married to a notorious outlaw, but the feeling had quickly worn off. They had no home life—he was never home—and she began to realize it would never change. Except that one day she would read that he had been shot and buried.

So she had packed her bags and departed.

Now she lived quietly, and none of her neighbors had any idea of her past. During the years she had lived as his wife he had been generous with money, and she had squirreled it away. When she left, she'd sold off the jewelry he'd given her, and sold their house. She was able to close her mind to the source of the money, and she was able to get by in Puente.

She never wanted to see him again.

★

Chapter 14

But Fate had one more wrinkle for her brow.

Frances was still a handsome woman and had a male friend, Walter Madsen, who was very attentive. He thought she was a widow. She had never told him about Pug or her life with him. She had no idea what that knowledge would do to their understanding . . . which was progressing very nicely. Walter was beginning to hint at marriage, and Frances was worrying about what to do. Should she go ahead and marry him and hope that it was never discovered? It might be the only answer.

And then Pug showed up.

He had the sense to come in at night and put his horse in the stable beside her buggy. She cried, seeing him, and asked him to go, but he would not. He slept in the stable that night.

She actually thought of going out after he was asleep and putting a bullet into him; but she was afraid of him. If she missed, he might kill her. If what she read in the papers was true, one more killing would be nothing to him.

She also feared for Walter.

He learned about Pug very quickly, and she was slightly surprised that he did not recognize Pug. His picture had been in the periodicals often enough.

"He's a cousin," she told Walter, "and not very stable in the head. Don't rile him up."

"What's he doing here? What does he want?"

"He—he was passing by," she said lamely.

To Pug she railed, "You can't stay here! I've got another life now! It doesn't include you."

"You're still my wife, dammit!"

"Please—I don't want anyone to know it! You're an outlaw!"

"You knew that when you married me."

"But it was all different then. I was young and foolish. Now I just want to live in peace. Go away, Pug!"

"I got money," he said. "Lots of money. I need a place to stay for a while. I'll pay you plenty to put me up."

That was a strong argument; she wanted the money. But she wanted Walter too, and what would he do if she let Pug stay in her spare bedroom? Cousin or no cousin, he would raise the roof!

Pug continued to sleep in the stable, and Walter complained, seeing his horse. "He's still here!"

"I-I-I can't make him leave! He's very stubborn—but he'll go of his own accord one day soon."

Walter grumped. "I don't want him hanging around here."

"I don't either . . . but he's not harming me."

"Nevertheless, I want him gone. I'll go talk to him."

"No, no, please, Walter! Stay away from him! He's dangerous!"

94

But Walter was a big, strong man. Pug was short and didn't look dangerous. In the stable he smiled and listened to Walter, then told Walter to go piss up a rope.

Walter reddened. He swung from the floor, a powerful fist to Pug's face—but never connected. Instead he staggered back as Pug fired into his chest, a single shot into the heart. Walter was dead before he hit the floor.

Hearing the shot, Frances came running from the house and found Pug standing over the body, reloading the Colt.

She sagged against the door. "You've killed him!"

"He attacked me," Pug said matter-of-factly. "He was a damn fool, Fran. You're better off without him."

She knelt by the body, feeling for a pulse that wasn't there. She looked up at Pug with hate in her eyes. "You're going to pay for this, Pug Bennett . . ."

He smirked. "I heard that b'fore."

"You come here and destroy my life! You kill everything you touch. Get out of here, Pug! Get away from me!"

He stared at her. She was serious. She jumped up suddenly and ran at him, her fists beating at him. He easily pushed her away and slapped her hard. She fell in a tangle of skirts and tried to get up, and he hit her again. Damn fool woman!

But he was through here. He saddled his horse and swung aboard, looking down at her. She was a big disappointment to him. He shook his head and rode out.

He was a long way from Otillo, but maybe he should go back there, as a hideaway. Coming to Puente had been a washout. You couldn't go back to a woman once you'd left her, huh? Tipo had told him that, hadn't he?

Ki nosed through all the saloons in Otillo, listening to the talk, contributing very little. He did strike up a conversation now and then and brought it around to Pug Bennett, but he learned nothing much. No one knew anything he didn't already know. They knew what they'd read in the papers.

They talked about Tipo, whom a lot of people had known, especially the girls. He had been generous with his money. The girls were sorry as hell he was gone.

Ki said to Jessie, "So of the four men who went into the Hatfield Bank, only Pug survives."

"The deadliest one."

"Yes, but he's not here in Otillo. He's probably holed up somewhere, growing another beard."

"He could be." She nodded slowly. "Maybe we ought to put out a poster showing him both ways, with the beard and without it."

"Good idea. As soon as we get back to civilization . . . which I think we ought to do. We're wasting our time here."

Pug arrived in Otillo late at night, put his horse in Tango's stable, and went upstairs; the saloon was closed, but Tango was still up, working on his ledgers. Pug went into his office and Tango set out a bottle.

"Is it a celebration or a wake?"

"Both," Pug said. He counted out Tango's cut of the robbery. "This is the celebration, but I suppose you've heard about Tipo?"

"Yes, we heard. Too bad." He poured drinks from the bottle and swept the money into a drawer. "What're you going to do now?"

"Go to Hollings and shoot the son of a bitch who killed Tipo."

Tango smiled. "He made a mistake, claiming the reward." They touched glasses. "Here's to his last rites." They drank, and Tango put the bottle aside. "So you saw Frances?"

Pug grunted and sighed. "She's not the same woman she was. Settled down like a goddam potted plant. Wouldn' take me in." He shook his head. "What the hell gets into wimmin anyways?"

"They're very peculiar."

"That's a fact."

Tango said, "This Benny Kubik is described as a saloon owner in Hollings. But he shot Tipo in Ryesburg. Does that mean he followed you two there?"

"It got to mean that, don't it?"

"Then he wanted to kill you too. There's a bigger reward for you than Tipo."

Pug nodded, frowning. "Yeah . . . But I didn't know who it was then or how many . . . so I slid out."

"The papers said there was a second man with Kubik."

"But it was Kubik who shot Tipo. Like you said, he made a mistake, claimin' the reward. Now I know who he is and where he is."

"Lay up a day'r two, Pug, rest."

"Yeah, I will."

In the saloon that night, Pug met Joey Norris. He was a bright-looking lad who, Tango said, had been involved in some midnight cattle deals and wide-loop horse trading. Tango thought he might be ready for bigger things. He was a quick learner and eager to meet Pug.

Tango had said earlier, "You need some partners, Pug."

"Yeah, I do . . ."

"Take Joey along when you go to Hollings. Break him in."

"Might do just that . . ."

In preparation for the trip, Pug took Joey out into the hills and set up a row of stones on a flat log as targets.

"Let's see you shoot, kid."

Joey proved to be a so-so marksman. He was not quick and not accurate with a pistol, though he tried hard.

"I never had the money to buy cartridges, Pug," he said. "Never could practice."

"You got to learn to use the sights. You just pointin' the damn gun."

He was a little better with a rifle but would never be a gunslick. He seemed an easygoing type, not overly talkative, and was obviously happy to be riding with Pug.

They would leave for Hollings the next day, Pug said. Maybe the kid would improve.

★

Chapter 15

Jessie and Ki, in Hatfield, heard nothing of Pug Bennett. It was as if the man had walked off the edge into nothingness. He had disappeared. The newspapers, which were so eager to print sensational stories about him, had about dried up.

Eastern papers, however, continued to print "news" purporting to be of Pug. They called him the Wild Man of the Plains, and mentioned the many notches on his gun. Apparently Easterners believed every Western badman notched his pistol for each killing, as if he had only one gun and kept it forever.

Pug lived a violent life, Jessie said, so maybe someone had centered him and left the body out in the sticks. Ki thought that if someone had shot him, knowing who he was, they'd want to collect the reward. After all, a thousand easy dollars was not to be ignored.

They discussed going to Hollings, where Benny Kubik had a saloon, wondering if Pug would go there to avenge

Tipo. Ki thought he would. Since the details of the shooting had been published in all the papers and many had talked about it in editorials, Ki thought it likely Pug Bennett would not be able to resist.

But of course Pug would not advertise his presence, being the sort of snake he was; he'd come into town secretly, shoot or stab Kubik, and sneak out before anyone knew he'd been there . . . Ki said.

Jessie asked, "Then why go there? Would we know any better than anyone else when he came in secret?"

"We'd be closer to the crime. If he goes there."

"If," she said.

Ki smiled. "Of course it's an *if,* but I think it's a strong one. How can Pug allow Kubik to live? It goes against everything he stands for."

Jessie laughed. "You mean viciousness and evil."

"Yes, of course."

"All right. You've talked me into it. Maybe we'll get lucky."

Pug and Joey Norris rode into Hollings well after dark, left their horses on a side street, and approached the Slipper cautiously. Pug did not want to be seen—and remembered. But there were very few people on the main street, which was not lighted.

Joey, who had never been in the town before, went into the saloon to make sure Kubik was there. And he was, behind the bar with another bartender, serving drinks.

Joey put one foot on the rail, sipped his drink, then wandered out. "He's there," he told Pug. "What you gonna do?"

"He killed Tipo for the bank money Tipo was carryin'. So we'll take that money away from him."

Joey's eyes widened. "You mean go in and hold him up?"

"No, I don't." He led the way back to their horses. "We'll camp out somewheres. Then in the morning you come in town and buy a gallon of coal oil. We going to burn him out. We'll fix 'is wagon."

Joey was startled. "You do that and you'll burn down the town!"

Pug pretended great surprise. "Izzit *your* town, kid?"

"No . . ."

"Then we'll burn it."

It was the middle of the week, and the town was very quiet after midnight. Everything was locked up, and most of the citizens were long since in bed asleep. Pug and Joey splashed coal oil along the three sides of the Slipper Saloon; it had a common wall with the store on the fourth side. The paint had been weathered off the siding years before; the dry wood drank up the lamp oil greedily.

Then Joey brought the horses, and Pug mounted and flipped a lighted match into a puddle that flared up instantly. As they rode away, the flames encircled the building happily, roaring in delight, feeding on the crackling wood like a monster hungry for raw meat. Grinning, Pug and Joey left the town behind.

They were half a mile away before they heard the fire bell, ringing like a mad thing.

"They ain't never going to git that out," Pug said.

"I thought you said you was going to shoot Kubik."

Pug nodded. "They's plenty of time for that later. He got to suffer a little bit first." He raised his voice to the surrounding darkness. "Tipo, if you's watching, this is for you!" He shook his fist in the direction of the fire.

He reined in and looked back. The fire was now a conflagration; obviously many buildings were involved. Flames and embers were shooting high into the dark sky.

"Kubik lost his shirt," Pug said with satisfaction. There was always the chance that he hadn't gotten out before the fire reached him. Pug savored the idea that he'd been trapped somewhere in an upper floor. Roasted Kubik! Pug laughed uproariously.

Jessie and Ki arrived in Hollings two days after the fire. The local lawman told them he was positive the fire was a case of arson. He had found an empty tin near what was left of the saloon. It had contained coal oil.

"Somebody burned the saloon—and didn't care about the other buildings downwind."

"It sounds like Pug Bennett's work," Ki said.

The Slipper was a blackened pile of smoldering ashes, and so were the five buildings that had abutted it to the north. The volunteer firemen had managed to get the fire under control at a side street, or half the town would have gone up. They had been lucky it had been a calm, misty night.

But Benny Kubik had lost everything he owned.

He had barely gotten out with his pants—and he didn't have the money he'd stolen from Tipo's body. He had put it into a safe on the second floor. The safe was now molten metal and everything inside burned to a crisp.

The next day, when people began to attach blame, Pug Bennett's name was mentioned very quickly, and no one seemed very sorry at Benny's predicament. He had brought it on the town, they said, by shooting Tipo. No one had seen Pug in the vicinity, but he was considered the cause of the calamity by nearly unanimous vote. Who else fit the circumstances half so well?

Benny had to beg money for breakfast.

The offices and printing press of the weekly were on the opposite side of the street and so escaped the flames. Jessie

102

and Ki talked to the editor-owner, Jonathan Weller. Weller was of the opinion that Bennett had set the fire. "It's the kind of thing a man like him would do for revenge."

Ki said, "I'd have thought he'd want to shoot Kubik. It's his usual method of solving problems."

"Yes, I'm sure he does." Weller smiled. "And he may do that at any time of course. Benny Kubik is trying to sell the land—the land that's under what used to be the saloon. When he does that, he says, he'll go back east."

"I would advise him to," Jessica said. "Even before he sells it."

"Yes, I too."

They did not talk to Kubik, who was drowning in self-pity, telling all who would listen that Pug Bennett had set the fire and that a posse should be formed to go after him.

"Which way?" someone asked.

"Out there," Kubik said, gesturing vaguely.

Jessie and Ki returned to Hatfield, and Jessie sat in the hotel for several days with her correspondence. Then one evening, as she and Ki were entering the restaurant, Charlie appeared.

"Charlie!" she said. "Is it really you?"

He approached them, a big grin on his face. "Hello . . ."

She took his hand. "Is the law close behind you, Charlie?"

"No, no, I swear it!" He held up both hands in denial.

Ki said, "Come and have dinner with us."

"Of course."

He had been in a dozen towns since he'd seen them, he said when they were seated, and had about given up the blue sky stock business.

"You've joined the church?" Ki suggested.

He laughed. "Nothing as drastic as that. But the stock business is getting riskier." His smile was rueful. "I've been shot at twice on leaving town too slowly. I think I'll get into something safer."

"You could rob stagecoaches," Jessie said.

His brows rose. "Please! I was actually thinking of something honest!"

"This *is* serious," Jessie agreed. "What were you thinking of?"

"I'm sure I could be a reporter."

"A reporter!"

"Yes indeed. I have friends on a Kansas City newspaper. I wrote to one of them, an editor, and he said to come and see him next time I'm in town. So of course I'm heading that way."

"You ought to be very good at it," Jessie said warmly. "You're good at talking to people, and that's what a reporter does, talk to victims and such . . ."

He grinned at her. "At least I could sell 'em a newspaper. After stocks, that ought to be easy."

A waiter took their orders, and when he had gone, Charlie said, "The gossip is that you're closing in on Pug Bennett. Is it true? Maybe that could be my first story as a reporter."

"It's not true that we're closing in," Ki said. "He's slippery as warm ice."

"We think he burned down part of Hollings, a town south of here." Jessie touched his arm. "That's supposition. We have no proof, so don't put it in your story."

"Why do you think he burned it?"

"To get at the man who killed one of his gang. You must have read about it . . ."

"No, I haven't read anything for more than a week. Where is Bennett now, d'you think?"

"Nobody knows. The man killed at Hollings was the last of his bunch—the ones who robbed the bank here in town and killed two people. We suppose he's recruited new hardcases."

"I wouldn't be surprised." Charlie smiled at them. "It's so good, running into you two. I almost feel that I'm home."

"And it's good to see you, Charlie," Jessie said. "Especially now that you're about to enter upon the straight and narrow."

"It makes me nervous," he admitted. "But I hope to get the hang of it. One thing—it'll be nice that I don't have to keep looking over my shoulder for an irate customer with a shotgun."

She laughed. "Or a sheriff."

Their steaks came, and they talked about Otillo and the No Man's Land strip, telling Charlie what they'd done. He had been to that part of the country once, he said, but preferred more settled regions. Then, after coffee, Ki said he had things to attend to and left them together.

He had intended taking the morning stagecoach, Charlie said, but now he'd decided to wait a bit. "I can always get on a stage . . ."

They lingered for a long while over coffee and, when the restaurant finally closed, strolled outside to sit on chairs along the warped boardwalk. Charlie wanted to hear more of their chase after Pug Bennett.

He disagreed with the idea that Pug might have picked up and run off to far places. "He knows you're after him and he'll blame you for the deaths of his gang members. He'll want revenge."

"He came after us once and lost Windy. You think he'll try it again?"

"Of course he will. He's a vicious killer. Don't let your guard down for a minute."

She said, "I doubt if he knows where we are."

"He may know more than you think. Assume he does, anyhow. He's vicious and ruthless, but he's not stupid. Be afraid of him . . . and by that I mean, watch your back!"

She squeezed his hand. "I will. You think revenge is that strong in him?"

"Absolutely. It may even be an obsession—something he *has* to do. He may not be able to live, knowing you and Ki are alive too."

She looked at him with raised brows. "Aren't you overstating it?"

Charlie shrugged. "I don't think so. Remember I've spent my life among people like Pug Bennett. I've heard their threats and boasts and I know something of the way they think. I've seen some of their threats carried out. I'm sure that sooner or later Pug will try to kill you two, and he won't do it openly. He'll shoot you from behind when you least expect it."

That was disturbing. And it meant she and Ki were locked in a feud that would doubtless last until one side or the other was dead.

Charlie went upstairs with her and kissed her good night at her door. "Lock it good."

He did not notice Ki, who watched from his own door as Charlie left to go downstairs again. Then Ki silently glided along the hall and tested Jessie's door to make certain it was securely bolted from the inside.

Their rooms were on the second floor, and he had already noted that Jessie's window faced a sheer drop to the hard ground. There was no way to climb up other than on a ladder, and bringing a ladder to the window would make a horrendous noise.

And a man climbing that ladder would make a fine target.

And Jessie was a dead shot.

106

★

Chapter 16

A fair was being held in a neighboring town, Raines, Charlie said. "Let's join the festivities."

She touched his nose with a finger. "You were just telling me to be careful, to watch my back."

He nodded. "And I still mean it. But Pug isn't going to shoot you in a group of your friends. He'd have to get too close and he'd be dead in a second too. That wouldn't appeal to him."

"Then let's go."

"A group is going to the fair in the morning. We can go with them."

Jessie discussed it with Ki, who agreed with Charlie. "It ought to be safe enough. We have three pairs of eyes to keep watch." He smiled. "And there's a third reason."

"What's that?"

"You could die of boredom here in Hatfield, where the most exciting thing to be seen in months is someone painting a fence."

She laughed. "You're right. I've already begun to notice it. Let's go to the fair."

It was a certainty, Ki said, that the hotel in Raines would be full to overflowing. "Why not hire a buckboard to carry what we need? It's only half a day's drive."

Charlie agreed, and they rented a light wagon from the livery. The owner loaned them a small tent. "For the lady . . ."

There were more than two dozen people bound for the fair. They met in the center of town, some with wagons, and set out, all in jovial moods.

Charlie drove the buckboard's two mules with Jessie beside him on the seat, with a parasol. She was in a dress for the occasion, her pistol in a shoulder bag. Ki rode alongside on a sorrel horse.

The weather was also in a good mood, giving them a gentle breeze that blew the dust of the road away across the flats and kept the sun's rays mild.

Ki was right; they reached Raines in half a day and found a place to camp in the fields, not far from the fair's entrance gate.

Raines was a slightly smaller town than Hatfield, and it hosted a small fair. But to people hungry for entertainment, it provided excitement, something different in their humdrum lives. Just to be among crowds of people was exciting.

Charlie and Ki pitched the tent beside the wagon and tied the mules and the sorrel on the edge of the camp area, where a picket line had been established.

Just inside the entrance gate, as they arrived, a wedding was in progress, a girl in white and a young man in a store suit that did not fit. When they were pronounced man and wife, the man yelled with his friends and lifted the girl into a light spring wagon, and they were off, out the gate at a run as the wedding crowd tossed old shoes after them and shouted advice, some of which made the parson frown as he pocketed his dollar.

The fair had one long "street" with concession stands on each side. They were makeshift booths, and the paint was not yet dry on some. Charlie bought them corn dodgers and they ate as they strolled, pausing to watch balancing acts and loud and racy puppet shows.

At the end of the street there were platforms built with side ropes; a sign advertised wrestling to be held later, husking bees and cockfights. Beyond was an oval for horse racing, where a dozen or more horses were moving about as men shouted at them.

To one side was a shooting gallery. Charlie urged Jessie to shoot. "You can win a prize!"

"I don't want to be singled out."

He sighed. "Maybe you're right. It might wind up in a newspaper. Can Pug read?"

"I'm sure he can."

"That's a shame. He probably spent a year in a school somewhere. Schools shouldn't allow outlaws in them."

She laughed. "You're silly, Charlie."

"Yes, I know. It's part of my charm. I'm afraid you'll have to put up with it. Where do you suppose Ki's got to?"

She glanced around. "He's probably looking into things. Ki's like a cat. He wants to see how everything works and what everyone does. By the end of the day I'm sure he'll know more about the fair than the people who run it."

"Not much gets past him?"

"Nothing gets past him," she said definitely.

"I'd better watch my Ps and Qs."

Jessie laughed again and squeezed his arm. "If he didn't like you, you wouldn't be here." She pouted. "Aren't you going to buy me some ice cream?"

"Of course." He went to a booth and came back with two cones, one of which he gave her. She licked it and looked at the sky. "It'll be dark soon. Maybe we ought to go back to the wagon."

"Yes. Maybe Ki will be there."

"No, he isn't."

He gazed at her in mild surprise. "He's not? How do you know?"

She patted his cheek. "Because he's right behind you."

Pug Bennett and Joey Norris had headed eastward, and the glow of the Hollings fire had been on the horizon for hours. Pug stopped several times to admire it. He had only one regret, which he did not share with Joey, that Tipo's money, stolen by Kubik, had burned up with everything else. Maybe he should have made an attempt to go in and get it from Kubik.

Hell, he could always set the place afire.

Hindsight was never wrong, was it?

Joey was grinning from ear to ear. He had never seen such a big fire before in his life. Privately he wished they could stay nearby and watch it burn. It stirred something in him.

When they finally came in sight of a town, it was on a railroad and Pug halted to look it over from a distance. "They on the telegraph," he said, pointing to the poles that marched away alongside the rails. "They'll know all about the fire b'now."

Joey said, "You want I should ride in?"

"Yeah. Get us some vittles and a newspaper, but don't call no attention to yourself. Don't be in a hurry. I'll wait right here."

"All right . . ."

"You're just a drifter. Don't get into no gab fests."

"Yeah, Pug."

The place was hardly a town. It was built around a water tower where trains stopped to take on great gulps of liquid. Sometimes passengers got off or on, but mostly not. It was called Packer's and had one deadfall, several small stores, and a few shack houses. Joey bought tobacco, some vittles, and a day-old newspaper. A stack of them had just arrived that morning, the storekeeper said. He was reading one himself.

When Joey returned to Pug, it was dark. They built a tiny fire in a ravine and ate beans and near-stale bread. Pug read the paper. There was nothing in it about the Hollings fire, he said, but he was pleased to learn that he was considered one of the most wanted badmen in the territory and his price had gone up two hundred dollars. He was now worth twelve hundred dollars, dead or alive.

It put him in a very good mood, but it did not occur to him that though he was moving up in criminal circles, he was still eating near-cold beans out of a can and sleeping on the ground.

When they hit Lamar, Pug walked his horse through the town at night, paying special attention to the bank. It was small, nestled between a shoe store and a photographer's shop. A side street was only three doors away. It led to some jumbled country that Pug thought was an excellent getaway route.

He and Joey camped at the edge of town and rode through it again in daylight. Pug got down and changed some money at the bank, looking it over, liking what he saw. It had only one guard and two tellers. When he went in, the guard was sweeping out, his shotgun twenty feet away.

He didn't really need money; he still had plenty, but Joey had none. Anything they bought came out of Pug's pile and Joey was embarrassed by it, he said. He wanted to take the bank so he could pay his own way.

"We'll take it," Pug said that night, "then go back to Hollings."

"Back there?"

"That son of a bitch Kubik is still on my list, kid. He kilt Tipo and I going to settle with him. Then I'm going to point for Texas."

"How much will we get from the bank?"

"They don't look prosperous. Maybe a couple thousand. We take what we can get."

Joey didn't think that was so bad. When you have nothing, a thousand is a fortune.

They rode into town just before the bank opened; its hours were posted on the door: 10 AM to 4 PM. They got down and talked for a few minutes while several customers hurried in and came out again.

Then Pug said, "Let's go. No shooting unless we got no damn choice. It'll wake the town."

Pug stepped inside and drew his pistol, pointing it at the guard, who stared at him, mouth hanging open. Pug motioned him and the tellers into a side room and closed the door, telling them to stay put. Then he and Joey piled all the money they could find into a gunnysack and hurried out to climb on their horses. Pug kept the sack.

As they rode away, someone inside the bank emptied a pistol, and Pug swore, seeing startled faces turned toward him and Joey. He spurred his horse as men ran into the street behind them and began firing.

Joey's horse went down in a tangle of legs.

Pug did not hesitate, but kept going, leaning far over as the horse ran flat out along the side street and left the town behind. Too bad about the kid. But if he'd stopped, they'd have had him too. He couldn't afford to stop, not with his record.

112

He reached the broken country and reined in to look back. No one was pursuing—but they would be. He went on at an easier pace, glancing at the sky. Hours and hours before dark. He patted the gunnysack. Now he had it all. Poor Joey; his luck was terrible.

He turned off the road in a dry creek bed where his horse left no tracks, and headed west. He did not stop that day and at night made a cold camp in an arroyo near some low hills. He had probably given a posse the slip.

Before he drifted off to sleep it occurred to him to wonder what had happened to Joey.

When his horse was hit and went down in the street, Joey had rolled free and had the sense to lay motionless on his stomach. Out of the corner of his eye he was able to see Pug galloping away to safety. Pug had not hesitated one second. He had been in the lead, but he must have heard the horse stumble and fall.

When he was surrounded, and one citizen was poking him with a rifle barrel, Joey sat up and they pulled him to his feet. Somebody took his gun and slapped his pockets while others examined the dead horse.

One said, "Ain't no money on him. T'other'n got it all."

A man with a star pinned to his shirt pushed him along to the jail as a posse was organized. A second deputy led it out of town. Joey was locked in.

"What's your name?" the man with the star asked.

"Joe Smith."

"Smith, huh? You damn sure it ain't John Doe? Who was the other one with you?"

Joey took a long breath. He sat on the iron cot dejectedly. Pug hadn't made one single move to help him. "Pug Bennett," he said.

"Bennett! I be piss damned!" The deputy stared at him a minute, then strode out, slamming the office door. Joey sat in the dark feeling sorry for himself. They hadn't shot anybody, so they wouldn't hang him . . . That was some small consolation.

The deputy was gone about a half hour, then returned suddenly. He stood in front of the cell. "That *was* Pug Bennett all right! We got two witnesses seen him."

"I told you," Joey said.

"He's worth twelve hunnerd dollars. You ain't worth a damn."

Joey sighed. "He talked me into comin' along with him."

"Where's he likely to go from here?"

Joey looked at the deputy with more interest. For the first time he wondered about a deal. Of course they wanted Pug! He said, "I know exactly where he's going."

"Oh? Where's that?"

"I know where he's going from here, and where he's going after that."

The deputy was silent a moment, staring at him. He glanced around at the other empty cells. "What's your real name?"

"Joey Norris."

"How long you been ridin' with Bennett?"

"Not very long. Since he lost a partner over to Ryesburg."

The deputy nodded. "We heard about that. Where's Bennett going?"

Joey eyed him. "What if you was to let me outa here?"

The deputy fished for a cigar and rolled it in thick fingers, frowning at his prisoner. "You want a deal, izzat it?"

"You said I wasn't worth a damn. You want Bennett."

"All right. You can tell me for sure certain where he's headed?"

"Damn right."

114

"He knows we got you, sonny. Maybe he won't go there."

Joey made a face. "He don't know if I'm dead or alive. He seen my horse go down is all. Besides, I know for sure he'll go there. He got a reason."

"A gal, huh?"

"He got a reason."

The deputy struck a match on the bars and lighted the cigar. He stared at Joey and blew smoke for a minute. "I'll think on it." He headed for the office.

Joey said quickly, "Don't think too long or he won't be there no more."

The deputy closed the office door and sent a boy to find Matt Brinton, a local hardcase handy with a gun. He sat in a chair and frowned at the street till Brinton arrived, a lean, dark man the same size as the deputy.

"What you want, Will?"

"I got the kid locked up who robbed the bank with Bennett . . ."

"Yeah . . . I heard."

"You throw in with me if I go after Bennett?"

Matt was surprised. "You know where he is?"

"The kid is goin' to tell me."

"We split even?"

"Down the middle."

"Sure, Will. When we leavin'?"

"In two hours. I got to talk to the kid again. He tells me where Bennett is and I let him out."

Matt whistled. "Can you trust 'im?"

Will shrugged. "Got to, don't I? Course, if he lies to me, ever' newspaper from here to Frisco will know he squealed on his partner. They tell me Bennett can read."

Matt smiled. "Go talk to the kid."

★

Chapter 17

Joey was probably dead. Too much lead content. He'd seen the kid's horse go down and had an instant's glimpse of Joey lying like a sack of meal in the dusty street. Too bad.

They had come through a fusillade of bullets. Some of them must have ventilated the kid and hit the horse. Pug smiled. He had been in the lead, so the kid had probably taken a few meant for him. That was the way it ought to be.

And he had all the money. He waited till sunup to count it. He had a little less than three thousand dollars, about what he'd expected. He stuffed it into the saddlebags and made coffee.

He went on west, navigating by guess, aiming for Hollings. He'd use a rifle on Benny Kubik, then head for Otillo, lay up there for a spell, and use up some of the money playing with the girls. It was time for a spree.

He hadn't had one for a long while, and he'd have this one with Joey's cut.

He said aloud to the space between the horse's ears, "I vote to use Joey's money."

Nobody voted against it.

Deputy Will Hanes opened the cell door and sat on the cot next to Joey. "All right, kid, you got a deal. You tell me all you know about Pug Bennett and you walk outa here."

"With a horse and my gun . . ."

"I give you your gun back, but the horse is up to you. If I let you have a horse, I got to account for it. You unnerstand I got to keep my hands clean."

"Yeah. But I get a horse?"

"The town's fulla horses. You're breaking jail tonight. Somehow you picked the lock and skedaddled—and stole a horse to boot. You foller'n me?"

"Sure."

"And you get the hell outa my jurisdiction."

Joey smiled. "I got it."

"And keep your mouth shut. We never had no deal, nothing at all."

"Yeah, all right."

"Good. Now where's Bennett?"

"He's on his way to Hollings to shoot Benny Kubik. Kubik shot Tipo, and Pug swears he'll center Kubik—and he will. After that, he's going down to Texas. Santone, I think."

"Anything else?"

"He got friends in the Strip—I guess you know that."

"You mean down in Oklahoma Territory?"

"Yes. Town called Otillo. He holes up there. Lots of hardcases do."

117

The deputy nodded. "I heard about that place." He got up. "We got ever'thing straight?"

"Yeah, all set. When d'I leave here?"

"Be smart to leave about midnight when everybody is in bed."

"Where am I goin' to get a horse?"

"There's corrals outside of town. Take your pick." The deputy went out and closed the cell door without locking it. "Don't tell me where you're going." He waved and went into the office.

Ki was nowhere around when Jessie and Charlie went back to the tent and crawled inside, fastening the flaps. They could hear people all around them, settling down, talking in low voices. Beyond, the sounds of the fair were constant—occasional shouts and the sharp, distant cracks of rifles and pistols at the shooting gallery. The racket would probably continue as long as there were people on the street.

It was pitch black in the tent. Charlie slid his arms about her and kissed her over and over again as though unable to get enough. She finally pushed him away to get her breath. Her hands wandered into his woolen shirt, and he ran his seeking hand down over her rounded hip.

She quickly unbuttoned her dress and deftly undid the buttons of her jacket. He slipped the gown off her shoulders, kissing her neck and ears . . . Jessie tugged at her petticoats and camisole as he helped her peel them away from her creamy skin until she was naked.

His eager hands explored the perfection of her breasts and the wonderful curve of her tiny waistline as she sighed in delight.

Then he tore at his jeans, yanking the buttons open, and kicked off his boots. Her questing hand captured his swollen member, caressing it seductively as she tried not to moan

118

aloud as his lips moved deliciously from one taut nipple to the other.

He slid atop her, and her legs came up, encircling his body as she guided the invader to its lair. She caught her breath, feeling it plunge deeper and deeper . . . She had to cover her mouth with a hand lest she inform everyone within earshot of their frantic tryst. The tent was only cotton cloth . . .

He moved and thrust; she writhed, and they rolled from side to side, panting and gasping—then suddenly halting all movement as voices spoke, seemingly only inches away, as several people stumbled along in the dark, seeking their own wagon. They were obviously not entirely sober, and one of them tripped over a tent peg and fell, swearing a blue streak almost in Jessie's ear.

Charlie snickered in her neck, moving again, and she slapped his butt. Then he began kissing her and she rubbed her heels on his back. She muffled her cries of ecstasy, her body pulsing and throbbing as he drove himself deep . . . then shuddered, holding her tightly . . .

The fair lasted three days, and they left for Hatfield on the morning of the third day. When they got back, Jessie and Ki talked to Marshal Hacker at once, and he had what he called confusing news for them.

"Got a night wire. It seems like Pug Bennett and some young feller named Norris robbed the bank in Lamar. The kid got hisself captured, Bennett got away with all the cash, and then Norris broke jail."

Jessie asked, "What's confusing about it?"

"Well, I been and seen that jail. I sure don't see how some young feller could break out that easy. Nobody else has. The wire don't say what happened, but the whole damn thing got a smell to it."

Ki asked, "How much cash was involved?"

"Only a couple thousand. Less than three."

"That doesn't sound as if Bennett would be interested."

Hacker nodded. "It was him though. They got witnesses. I guess he thought it'd be a easy nut to crack. And it sounds like it was. They didn't hurt nobody in the bank, but Norris got grabbed."

The weekly had no more news of the robbery, however. Joe Norris, Pug Bennett's sidekick, had been captured when his horse was killed on the getaway. He had been jailed but had broken out the same night. A horse was also missing from a corral just outside town. Deputy Will Hanes told reporters that he'd been out of town at the time, investigating another crime, and he had no explanation for the break-out. Neither did the other deputy. There had evidently been a mix-up between the deputies; the second had thought Hanes was on duty at the jail, and Hanes had thought his partner was. But both men said that should have had no effect on the jail. Somehow the prisoner had picked the lock or had a key.

"Don't that sound fishy?" Hacker said, reading the paper. "It listens like somebody was paid off."

Deputy Will Hanes and Matt Brinton traveled to Hollings without delay. Hanes had pocketed his star—he was far out of his jurisdiction anyhow. They had the poster portrait of Bennett, and when they reached Hollings, they went from one saloon to the next watching for him . . . and not finding him.

A good section of the town was blackened by fire, but men were clearing the ashes, hauling away debris, and new buildings would go up soon, they were told.

Since Bennett was determined to shoot Benny Kubik, they located him. He was working in the Osage Saloon to make ends meet. He talked to them but refused to say where he stayed at night.

Yes, he said, he was afraid of Pug Bennett, when Will Hanes asked him. But he was taking precautions. He wore a sawed-off twelve-gauge double-barreled shotgun on a sling over his shoulder. He could swing it up in a second and demonstrated.

"I know exactly what Bennett looks like," he said. "He comes in here, and he gits this." He swung the scattergun up. "Both barrels." He grinned at them. "Then I collect the reward and build m'saloon again."

When they had gone out to the walk, Matt said, "Goin' in there is the last goddam thing Bennett is gonna do. He'll shoot Benny goin' in or comin' out . . . if he can find 'im."

Will agreed. Owlhoots like Pug Bennett were devious as hell. They seldom did what you figured they'd do. Joey Norris was positive that Bennett was on his way to Hollings, but he could be wrong—or lying. And maybe Bennett had decided to wait a few months till Benny let his guard down.

Pug Bennett was a short man, shorter than most, and had red hair, but Will Hanes was sure that he'd dyed his hair by this time. Red was such a giveaway. There were several hair dyes on the market; there was no reason why he wouldn't have done it. "He shaved his beard once that we know about . . . We got to expect his hair is dark now."

It was not easy to locate one man in an entire town, especially when that man didn't want to be found, and even though the town was small, like Hollings. Hanes and Matt Brinton looked closely at every short man they came across.

Will said a short man might build up his height an inch or two, so they looked at heels. An inch meant more in some places than others. The posters said Pug Bennett was five-feet-six in stocking feet.

They were in the town four days before they saw him.

Matt saw him first, coming out of a livery stable. He thought the man looked furtive, and they followed him to a house just off the main drag—a short hombre with dark hair.

"He lives in there," Matt said. "It got no sign on it, but it must be a boardinghouse."

"You sure it was Bennett?"

Matt was annoyed. "I been lookin' at that goddam pitcher for weeks! I put my hand on the book, it was him."

"What you think he was doin' at the livery?"

"How the hell I know? Maybe gettin' a horse plated."

"Umm. That's likely. But we dassen't go in there," Will said, staring at the house. "We'll have to wait till he comes out."

"It could be morning."

"We got to do it."

They found a hiding place across the street, behind some big trash boxes, where passersby would not notice them, and waited through the night. They were both miserable and grumpy by morning, stiff and vastly uncomfortable.

So when the short man appeared, neither one was willing to wait another second. As the man came across the street, Will got to his feet and waved his Colt. "You under arrest, Bennett."

"What?" The man stopped. "I ain't no Bennett."

Matt growled at him. "Lay down. We goin' to tie you."

The man scowled, and his hand shot inside his coat and came out with a pistol.

Both Will and Matt fired, and kept firing.

The man crumpled and fell, a bloody mess, kicking a few times, then still.

They looked down at him, reloading. Will said, "Of course he'd say he wasn't Bennett . . ."

Matt turned the head around. "Lookit him. He's Bennett."

The sound of firing drew a crowd that surrounded the fallen man, and one said, "That's Homer Gillespie!" He looked at Will and Matt. "Whad he do?"

"You know 'im?" Matt said.

"Ever'body in town knows 'im. He owns the barber-shop."

"Jesus!" Will said.

★

Chapter 18

Jessie's suggestion—printing posters of Pug Bennett with and without the beard—had long since been followed, but so far nothing had come of it.

Leon Hacker said, "People got their own problems. They ain't watching ever'one they meets to see if he's Pug Bennett or not. I figger we'll be lucky as hell if anyone spots him."

"And if they do," Ki said, "he will be far gone before we can reach the place. I agree that luck is going to play a large part in this—good or bad."

"He'll go somewhere to hole up, won't he?" Leon supposed. "He got the Lamar money now and no partner—unless this here Joey Norris hooks up with him again. He maybe got to break in a new man or two."

"That might mean Otillo again," Jessie said, and they looked at her.

Ki shook his head. "That's a very long ride on nothing but hope and suspicion."

"Then there's nothing much we can do," Jessie replied, "but wait for information."

"One thing—we could go to Lamar," Ki said, "and hope for something positive."

She smiled. "It's closer than Otillo. Why not?"

In due time Will Hanes and Matt Brinton were taken before the circuit judge and accused of shooting down the town barber without provocation.

"What's that mean, provocation?" Matt asked.

"It means you murdered him without a reason."

"Hell—we thought he was Pug Bennett!"

The judge, a fleshy-faced man with steel-rimmed specs, glared at them. "You consider that an excuse for crissakes? Pug Bennett is red-haired. All the posters say so. The man you shot had dark hair."

Will said, "We figgered Bennett would dye his hair, Judge. And this barber sure looked like him."

The judge had a poster and frowned at it. "Yeah, I admit he looked some like this pitcher . . ."

"And he pulled a gun on us!"

"He must've thought he was bein' robbed!" The judge slammed down his gavel. "All that aside, you two're guilty of shooting down a innocent citizen on the city street and there's no two ways about it. I am sentencing you both to two years in the territorial prison." He pointed the gavel at them. "I'm takin' account of the fact that Gillespie *did* look some like Pug Bennett, and givin' you the benefit of the doubt." He banged with the gavel again. "Call the next case."

Everyone in Hollings knew that the barber, Mr. Gillespie, had been shot to death when two strangers had taken him for Pug Bennett.

Pug Bennett heard it too. He was living in a shack several

125

miles outside the town and going each night, hoping to get a shot at Benny Kubik. He had quickly learned that Benny worked in the Osage Saloon, but he could not find out where he slept.

He very much enjoyed hearing about how the two strangers had accosted the barber and emptied their revolvers into him at point-blank range. It was delightful that one of the strangers had turned out to be a deputy sheriff from Lamar—and that he was now going to prison.

But underneath all of that, Pug was putting two and two together. What about Joey—had he spilled some beans?

Wasn't it curious that soon after Joey had been captured by the law, that same lawman had turned up in Hollings looking for him, Pug? And immediately Joey had broken out of jail?

It all added up to betrayal, didn't it? Joey must have sold him out.

But the law had made a mess of it, shooting the wrong man. Pug grinned in the night. Lady Luck was still on his side.

Except in the matter of Benny.

Where the hell did Benny spend his nights? Did he sleep in the saloon? That was probably it. Pug didn't dare enter the deadfall; he was certain Benny looked hard at every man who came through the batwings.

Could he take a chance and shoot at Benny from the door? He shook his head. There were too many in between, and Benny was always behind the bar. It would take one hell of a lucky shot. And it would warn Benny. Now Benny didn't really know if he was being watched or not.

But Pug couldn't watch both front and back doors at he same time. And he knew there was an inside stairway to the second floor. But he didn't know if Benny could get to the roof . . .

He was sure Benny was spooked by the murder of the barber, even though he knew it had not been done by Pug. He was sure to take plenty of precautions. Did he sleep in the saloon or not?

Pug felt very annoyed that he had to wait around to get answers to these questions. The longer he hung around the town, the more opportunities the law had of grabbing him. His freedom had always depended on movement. Sheriffs' jurisdictions ended, and communication between lawmen was usually poor. Pug depended on this—as did all owlhoots. If you kept moving, you usually stayed out of jail.

Now he wasn't moving. And it worried him.

Benny Kubik knew everyone in town; he'd lived in Hollings for two decades, after all. He told every customer and barfly who would listen that the notorious outlaw Pug Bennett was after him because he'd collected on the criminal Tipo as per the Wanted dodger.

That's why he carried the sawed-off, double-barreled artillery, and why he was usually sleeping in the saloon—though he got damned tired of being cooped up. He didn't like to sleep there, because the iron cot was hard and the mattress was thin and lumpy. When he protested to Zeke, the boss, Zeke told him to sleep on the floor.

Two of his friends had told him they'd seen a shadow lurking near the saloon late at night. The shadow might be Pug. Benny hated to take chances, so he stayed in the saloon.

But when he felt he could not put up with the damned cot any longer, he climbed upstairs to the roof, across it and the next two, and down into the alley via a window and a drainpipe. He slipped across the alley and into Mrs. Lisser's boardinghouse, quiet as a prowling cat.

The only danger was crossing the alley. But he wore dark clothes and went quickly in the pitch black, making no more sounds than a thought. He didn't even tell Zeke about Mrs. Lisser.

Benny's precautions paid off. He was not detected, not seen, and Pug finally gave it up. He was sick and tired of living in the old shack, avoiding everyone, especially girls. One morning he said "the hell with it," saddled his horse, and lit out for the Strip. Benny Kubik could go to hell. Benny's luck was better than his—in this respect anyhow.

Benny had no way of knowing Pug's decisions, and continued his precautions.

Then one night, as Benny was asleep in the saloon, he woke to the unmistakable sounds of someone breaking in. The intruder broke the glass of the rear window.

Benny let the unlucky would-be burglar have both barrels at medium range.

The heavy buckshot made a horrendous hole in the wall where the window had been and scattered the remains of someone—no one could ever identify the deceased— all over the alley. Was it Pug . . . or not?

Zeke said he was grateful to Benny for guarding the petty cash, but he insisted Benny sleep elsewhere thereafter. It cost him more to fix the hole in the wall than what he might have lost to a burglar.

Jessie and Ki arrived in Lamar and read in the paper about the trial of Deputy Hanes and Matt Brinton, held in Hollings. Both men had been hauled off to the territorial prison for fatally shooting a man they thought was Pug Bennett.

"The victim turned out to be a barber," Ki said, "and it says here he drew a pistol, but the judge still sent the two men to jail. The paper hints that they were not careful enough to make sure of the man's identity."

Jessie said, "I find it curious that a young man like Joe Norris could so easily break out of jail. And immediately afterward the same lawman is in Hollings, looking for Pug."

"Yes, it's remarkable. Marshal Hacker was probably right about the smell. That lawman was after the reward. And now he's in jail."

"And young Joey Norris is probably in St. Louis by this time. If he double-crossed Pug, he'll keep going."

Ki said, "Do you suppose Pug *was* in Hollings?"

She shrugged. "If he was, he's long gone. Let's hear what the bank manager has to tell us."

But he had little to say that was any help. Two men, one of them undoubtedly Pug Bennett, had come into the bank, disarmed the guard, and swept the available cash into a sack. And departed without firing a shot.

One of the tellers had emptied a pistol into the sky to alert the town after the robbers had gone, and Norris's horse had been killed.

"Too bad it wasn't Bennett instead," the manager said.

Summer, and subsequently Indian summer, had faded away into fall, and Pug was caught in a cold rainstorm, miles from any cover. He had to ride through it, cursing his luck, all the way into Otillo. When he arrived, he was soaked through, tired, and irritable, and even Tango's good humor could not bring him out of it.

He felt a bit better after a hot bath and warm clothes and a drink or two. Tango came to his room with a bottle and glasses, and they talked. Pug told him about Joey's double-cross, and Tango was aghast that anyone would commit such a crime. He had certain contacts in towns like Kansas City and St. Louis, he said. "I'll write to them and explain that Joey is no longer one of us . . . and not to be trusted. That should do it."

It helped to raise Pug's spirits.

Tango laughed heartily when he learned that the deputy and the other one, Brinton, had been sent off to prison for shooting a barber who happened to resemble Pug.

That accounted for two enemies, Pug said. But there was still the Chinaman who had killed Bob, and the blond girl. He had no idea where they were. He hoped they had given up the chase for the reward.

"Well, you're safe here, Pug," Tango assured him. "If those two show up, they're a distinctive pair. We'll take care of them."

Pug thanked him.

Chapter 19

Pug was born to be suspicious, and he had nurtured and developed that trait over the years. It helped him to stay alive. It seemed to him that Tango was going out of his way to be helpful. What did the man want?

Pug found out in the first week. Tango had another job planned and wanted him to carry it through.

"It's a large payroll," Tango said. "It's delivered in cash once a month by stagecoach."

"And the stage is guarded . . ."

"Yes, by horsemen and two men inside the coach."

Tango also had a map. He traced the route of the stage with a pencil. "It goes from here, on the railroad, a train stop called Newton, to here, the mine. It's about eighty miles away. The payroll is for the workers."

"How much money?"

Tango smiled. "My information says an average of seventy-five thousand dollars each month."

Pug whistled. That would be a haul! No wonder Tango

was pushing. He said, "We'll need some men . . ."

"I'll supply them. How many?"

"Maybe three. Lemme think it over." Pug frowned at the map. It didn't tell him enough. He would have to go there and look at the country. To find a good ambush spot for one thing. That kind of money deserved first-class treatment. He had never come near that much in one robbery.

He needed to rest up a few days, he told Tango, then go and see for himself what was involved—and how he would get out of there after the robbery.

Tango was eager for him to go, but he agreed on a short wait.

Pug had not had a woman in a long while. He looked over Tango's saloon girls and selected a dark-haired girl called Emma. He took her and a bottle to his room and gave her a drink.

She said, "You're Pug Bennett, huh?"

"Yeah, sure . . ."

She grinned at him. "How many men you killed?"

What the hell kind of a question was that! "What you wanna know for? You the goddam law?"

She giggled. "Yeah, you're under arrest."

He slapped her ass. She was pretty cute. "Hey, take off your dress."

She slid out of it casually. She had firm, pointed breasts and shook them at him, smiling, with a sidelong look. He pulled off his boots and tossed them aside.

Emma crawled naked onto the bed and sat cross-legged, while he pushed out of his jeans.

She said, "There's a big reward out for you, huh?"

"Sure. You wanna collect it tonight?"

She giggled again. "Wish I could. I'd go back t'New Orleans and buy me one of them pretty men and kick this life in the butt."

Pug chuckled at her language. "You don't like this life?"

She made a face and lifted one creamy shoulder. "It beats workin' in a factory—which I was doin' when I met Tango."

He climbed onto the bed and pushed her down. She grabbed his rampant member in both hands, jerking it hotly. Shoving her legs apart, he lowered himself as she rubbed the shaft on her furry nest. He guided it and pushed, and it entered her quickly, warm and tight.

He pushed it in deep, and she gasped and sucked in her breath. "Christ! You in a hurry. . . ."

He grunted, scooping her up, thrusting hard; he held her tightly till she slapped his arms. "Lemme breathe . . ."

He relaxed his grip but continued pounding her into the mattress. Damn it felt good . . . Did he want to go back out onto the cold prairie so soon? Why not wait a week or two and diddle around with Emma—or one of the other girls?

Why not?

Hollings was about the same distance from Lamar as Hatfield, so Jessie and Ki decided to go there again, where the shooting of the barber had taken place.

Benny Kubik was still working in the Osage Saloon with his shotgun handy. No, he said to Ki's question, he had not seen hide nor hair of Pug Bennett. But he was watchful and wary. "Just let 'im come in here . . ."

Jessie called on editor Jonathan Weller, but he had no news either concerning Bennett. "He's dropped out of sight. His kind thrives on publicity, so that's curious. I'm sure that the reward increase to twelve hundred pleased him enormously."

"Did the barber, Mr. Gillespie, really look like Pug?"

"Yes, he did, matter of fact. There was a strong resemblance, apart from the hair color. And they were about the same height. The two men who shot him must have been greedy for the reward. They apparently approached the situation carelessly, frightened poor Gillespie so that he reacted—and then they shot him. It was a shame."

Jessie said, "Benny Kubik expects Pug to show up here in Hollings."

"Yes, so I've heard. And I've been wondering how long Benny can last."

"What do you mean?"

"I mean the strain on him must be terrible. I imagine his nerves are about gone. He's constantly on the alert and that's sure to take its toll, isn't it? One of these days Benny is likely to explode!"

Her eyes widened. "Explode?"

"In one way or another. He's carrying that damned shotgun around everywhere . . ."

"I certainly agree he ought to leave Hollings. But maybe he's afraid to."

"He ought to leave here," Weller said. "One day we're likely to have another Gillespie case. Benny will see someone who he thinks resembles Pug Bennett and he'll start shooting." The editor sighed deeply. "In that crowded saloon—it could be a massacre."

"Who owns the saloon?"

"A man named Zeke Edwards. I've told him what I fear, but he doesn't agree. For one thing, Benny brings in trade. People want to stare at the man Pug Bennett is trying to kill."

Tango bought a half dozen newspapers from a passing traveler—his usual source of news—and he and Pug read them, starting with the earliest, which was only a month old.

And as he read, Pug began to notice one thing. Anoth-

134

er man was taking his place, and it apparently stemmed from the Lamar bank robbery. Too many newspaper scribes were calling it a two-bit job! They were making jokes about him—the notorious Pug Bennett holding up a little crackerbox bank, like a child stealing cookies. One writer even speculated that Pug was losing his nerve.

That struck too damned close to home!

The other owlhoot was named Bill Sands—some called him Dirty Bill. He and several others were raising hell in Missouri, robbing banks and trains. He had a certain flair, and the newspapers followed him closely in the finest tradition of yellow journalism. Pug Bennett was pushed off the front pages, to his disgust.

"Wait till you do the payroll job," Tango told him. "Then they'll forget all about Dirty Bill. He's never stolen half that amount."

That cheered him up. The payroll robbery, seventy-five thousand dollars, was bound to make headlines in every paper in the nation! Then they'd write about him with real respect!

Pug went down to the saloon in the morning before it opened for business. Tango had assembled a group of men for him to talk to and decide about. He figured three men would ride with him. That ought to do it.

Each man asserted he was experienced in the holdup dodge and capable. Pug talked with an even dozen and finally selected the three he thought would do.

But he took his time about deciding when they would go. In the meantime he spent his nights with Emma. She made them so pleasant he hated to hit the trail again, where he'd sleep alone on the ground and have to put up with the cold weather. It was winter, and the traveling would be harder. But when he mentioned putting the entire thing off till spring, Tango lost his smile.

"The mine might close down by then! This is the time to do it, Pug, when they'll never expect it!"

Of course he wàs right, but Pug hated to leave—and Emma hated to see him go—she said.

No one had seen Pug Bennett since the Lamar bank robbery—that they knew about. Ki suggested that maybe something happened to him. Summer was long gone, the winter rains shortened the days, and snow coated them. The chances were, Pug had holed up for the winter. He no longer had a gang anyhow.

Ki visited the Osage Saloon frequently and talked with Benny, who seemed about the same, still carrying the heavy artillery and still edgy. However, he had sold the land his saloon had been built on and was considering going east.

"I got the money for the fare . . ."

Ki urged him to go. Benny had relatives in Maryland whom he hadn't seen in many years.

Benny worried, "What if he holds up the stagecoach?"

"How is he going to know you're on the stage? He can't be everywhere," Ki argued. "Just make sure you don't advertise your going."

"I ain't mentioned it to a soul, 'cept you."

"Keep it that way. If you want, I'll go with you to the station."

"Yeah, thanks."

Benny made up his mind several days later, packed what he owned and told Ki, who went first to the stage station to look it over. He could find nothing suspicious. He put Benny on the Concord and said good-bye.

He watched the stagecoach roll out and take the road east.

That same week Charlie decided to go east himself, to Kansas City, to see his newspaper friend. He was embarrassed to be running out of money, but he would accept none from Jessie.

"That's a sign of my turning honest," he said to her. "A few years ago I would have given you stock in exchange for dollars and never thought twice about it." He laughed. "And I never would have paid you back, either."

"I'm proud of you and your new morals," she said. "Are you sure you've destroyed all those pretty stock certificates?"

"Every single one. That shady part of my life is gone forever."

"What if you don't make it as a reporter?"

"Then I'll go back to selling stock." He laughed at her expression. "No, I won't. But I refuse to consider that. I'm going to succeed as a newspaperman. And I intend to wind up owning the paper."

"Legally, I hope."

"I'll play by their rules."

She planned to go along with him to the stagecoach waiting room and see him off. He would go on the midday stage, he told her.

She was mildly surprised that he did not spend his last night with her, saying that he was sure if he did, he would never go at all.

So she slept alone, and in the morning found a note that had been slipped under her door. Charlie had taken the morning stage east. He hated good-byes, he wrote, so it was easier this way. He would never forget her, and the next time she was in Kansas City . . .

★

Chapter 20

Pug knew nothing about any of the men he'd selected, except what they told him. Of course Tango recommended each man, but what did Tango know about walking into a bank with a gun? He'd never done it. Tango's word about an accomplice was really worthless.

However, Pug could see that all three were toughs and could handle themselves. The oldest, and maybe most experienced, was Lem Danton, whom Tango said was wanted in Texas. He was gray and slit-eyed and spoke very little. The largest in bulk was Tim Foster, who told Pug at once that Foster was not his real name.

"My real name is on a piece of paper." He slapped his shirt pocket. "If I get dead, you see I'm buried under that name."

"I promise," Pug said. Jesus, the ideas some people came up with.

The youngest was Frank Linker, quick-eyed and deeply tanned. He seemed eager to please. They had all expressed

138

themselves as being eager to participate in a well-planned enterprise that would net each a tidy sum.

Pug explained that he was the leader and if any of them had reservations concerning that, he should step aside at once. None did. Tango had already assured them that Pug had luck on his side, and they were willing to let it rub off on them.

It had not rained for a week when Pug had the three draw straws to see who should accompany him to look over the route and select a bushwhack spot. Frank Linker drew the longest, and got his gear together. He and Pug rode out in the cold dawn, toward Newton.

It took days. They laid up a full day because of a violent rainstorm, and even when it let up, the going was very slow on muddy trails, crossing overflowing streams . . .

Frank proved to be talkative, always about girls. He jabbered about a girl in Denver and one in Fort Smith. He bragged about his experiences in a buckboard outside of Salina and in a cornfield nearby. Pug was sick of the sound of his voice long before they reached the little rail-road town.

Newton wasn't much; it was a water stop that had spread out a bit and now comprised a short street with a few stores and two saloons and the usual corrals and shacks, surrounded by a great deal of horizon.

The town had no hotel, so they slept in a stable, happy to be under a roof. In the morning Pug stayed out of sight, fearing he'd be recognized because of the damned posters, and Frank asked the questions: Is the mine hiring? How do I get there?

The mine, he learned, was owned and run by the Westhills Mining Company. They had a small hiring office next to the New Century Saloon.

There was apparently a big turnover of workers, Frank

told Pug. Men would stay for a week or a month, then leave. The road to the mine was well marked, starting at the edge of town.

It was a deeply rutted wagon road; they followed it for miles through low hills and flatlands. In late afternoon Pug halted as they approached a steep-sided hill that was perhaps thirty feet above the road. The road curved around it and continued. The top of the hill was thickly fringed with tall weeds and brush.

"This'll do," Pug said with satisfaction. "Four guns on top of that hill there. We shoot the mules and stop the wagon, and scatter the guards . . . Shouldn't be no trouble at all."

He led the way back down the road for half a mile, then rode through the brush and stunted trees to the top of the hill, where he dismounted and contemplated the road below. It came directly for the hill for several hundred yards before it curled around the steep slope.

Frank grinned. "Hell, they won't know what hit 'em."

"That's the idea."

Pug walked over and around the hill, looking for the best getaway route, and finally decided the way they'd come was as good as any. Of course if they did the job right from the hill, they wouldn't have to worry about getting away. There wouldn't be anybody alive to oppose them.

They would go back down the wagon road, then cut across country, heading west.

He climbed on his horse. "Let's go home."

They were lucky on the way back; it did not rain. When they arrived in Otillo, Tango had a week-old newspaper that had printed an item concerning the Westhills Mine. A mining engineer stated there was evidence the vein was about to play out. If that proved true, the entire shebang would have to be terminated. The engineer estimated the company would have less than two months to operate full blast.

"You'll have to hit 'em immediately," Tango said, "before they cut down the work force . . . and the pay-roll."

Pug groaned. It would mean he and the others had to go out there at once—and it had started to rain again. He bitched and swore, but it helped very little. Despite his opinions, the rain continued.

They got supplies together, packed them on a mule, and set out.

Sitting in the hotel lobby, reading a newspaper, Ki's eye fell on the item: The Westhills Mining Company might have to close down its mine in the territory, throwing a large number of men out of work. It was a large enterprise, employing round-the-clock crews.

The item mentioned that if the miners had to be laid off, it would mean a loss of some seventy-five thousand dollars a month to them.

Ki said to Jessie, "Here's a seventy-five-thousand-dollars-a-month payroll! Would that attract someone like Pug Bennett?"

"I'm sure it would. Let me see that paper . . ."

The article described the operation of the Westhills mine, really several connecting mines. At the location a small town had been erected, composed of worker's shacks, company stores and offices.

The bubble-headed reporter who wrote the story also mentioned that the workers were paid once a month in cash that came by wagon from Newton, a railroad town eighty miles away.

Jessica sighed. "If Pug reads this, I don't see how he could resist it."

"Should we warn the mine operators?"

"Wouldn't you think they'd have some kind of security system?"

"I would." Ki frowned. "But I think we should wire them at least."

"All right."

Ki rose. "I'll take care of it." He went out.

An answer from Westhills came in three hours. A vice president thanked them for their warning but assured them the mine security force was adequate.

"The wire has a kind of sarcastic bite to it," Ki said, handing the yellow sheet over. "Like mind your own business."

Jessie shrugged. "And so we will. For now."

It had stopped raining long before they reached the mine road out of Newton. According to Tango's calculations they were three or four days ahead of the usual payroll run.

The roadway was packed-down dirt but pristine. Nothing large had disturbed its surface since before the rains. Pug examined the road without setting foot on it. A few small animal tracks crossed it. Nothing else . . .

They rode parallel to the road, around the back of the steep-sided hill, and made camp. Pug selected four rifle positions on the brow, overlooking the road. The chances were, the guards would not even see them. As Frank said, they would not know what hit them.

Seventy-five thousand dollars!

A day later they watched as six well-armed mounted men passed the hill, heading toward Newton.

Pug said, "Those are probably the payroll guards. If Tango's right, they'll come back with a light wagon."

Tango's information was correct. They heard the wagon, iron tires on the gritty road, a long way off and slid into their positions with the rifles cocked.

The operation went exactly as planned, without a hitch.

142

Frank shot the two mules, halting the wagon, and Pug shot the driver off the box. Lem and Tim fired at the riders; only two got away.

None of the guards fired up at the hill. Surprise was complete. When the powder smoke cleared away, they went down the slope to find the wagon packed with supplies and three leather-topped, canvas sacks full of greenbacks.

"When the wagon don't arrive," Pug said, "they going to send out a party. We'll leave ever'thing as it is. Tie on them bags and let's be skedaddlin'."

They headed down the road. Pug figured they would be three, maybe four, days ahead of any pursuit.

When the news of the robbery came over the wire, Ki said, "I wonder how those officials at the mine feel now? They were warned and took no precautions . . ."

"They simply underestimated Bennett. Do you doubt it was Bennett?"

"Not me," Ki said. "According to the telegraph, two men escaped and went back to Newton. We ought to talk to them."

"I'll get my things together."

It was a three-day journey, moving as quickly as they were able, navigating with a map and considerable luck. They turned east when they reached the railroad tracks, on Ki's hunch, and it was proved out; they rode into Newton late the third night.

Only one of the survivors was still in Newton. Ki found him in one of the saloons with his arm in a sling. His name, he told Ki, was Elmer Perry. The second man who had escaped the outlaw's rifles was in Roseburg, forty miles east, where there was a hospital of sorts.

"I got hit along the arm, a kinda glancing shot," Elmer said, indicating the length of the wound. "But Gary got it

143

three times. None of 'em was real serious except he lost too much blood."

"Did either of you see any of the men who fired on you?"

"Not a damn one. It was a surprise. They opened up on us from a bluff. I seen the mules go down and the driver knocked offen the seat. Me and Gary yelled at each other and got the hell out as fast as we could go."

"Do you have any idea how many there were?"

"Four'r five, I guess. At the time it seemed like a goddam platoon! A hell of a lot of lead comin' at us. Me and Gary was lucky we was in the rear. They kilt ever'one else."

"And you saw none of them?"

"Hell, they wasn't any time for gawkin', mister."

Ki reported the conversation to Jessie. "It was a perfect ambush. The survivors saw no one."

Jessie had not been idle. She had made inquiries and turned up a man who claimed to be a tracker. His name was Jules Cortes, a middle-aged man getting stout about the middle. He had worked for the army for twenty years as scout and tracker, he told them, and had papers to prove it.

He was living in a house now, with his wife and two sons, and was not eager to get out on the trail again, having given up that hard life. But Jessie enticed him with gold, and he finally agreed to help.

They took the rutted road to the mine and halted just below the steep-sided hill where the bushwhacking had taken place. Asking them to wait, Jules climbed to the top of the hill. He was gone half an hour, and when he came back, he said he had found the outlaw's camp and probably their escape route.

"They went west from here," he said. "You want to follow them?"

"Yes." Jessie nodded.

It had not rained since the robbery, but the ground was damp and the tracks of four horses were deep and clear. Jules said, "They might as well have left a signboard."

Jessica nodded. "It looks as if they didn't worry much about being followed."

"Prob'ly not. They're days ahead of a pursuit, and as soon as it rains again, the tracks will be gone."

A posse had followed the outlaws for a day but lost the tracks. Jules showed them where the posse had milled around and finally gone back. "They gave it up."

The tracker pointed out the outlaws' campsites, but at the third one he hesitated and motioned them to stand clear. He got down and touched the ground with tentative fingers.

Ki asked, "What is it?"

"I don't know—something happened here . . ." Jules examined the earth with care, squatting, head down, his hat brim almost touching. He seemed to sniff the ground, moving slowly. He got to his feet and walked cautiously, bending double. He left them behind, disappearing from view in the brush.

When he came back, he was shaking his head.

"They split up here." He pointed west. "One man with all the horses went that way. He rode one and led the others. The other three men went west on foot."

Jessie said, "One man put them afoot!?"

Jules smiled and showed them an empty whiskey bottle. "Maybe he got them drunk—"

Ki nodded and tossed the bottle aside. "That would be like Pug Bennett."

Jessie said, "So he got away with the money . . ."

"And made it impossible for them to follow him."

★
Chapter 21

Pug Bennett had never been so close to a fortune before. His biggest haul had been slightly more than eighteen thousand dollars, and he'd had to split that with two partners in crime.

And it had been a long time ago.

But here he had more than seventy thousand dollars in cash in his keeping! That much money would settle him for life! He would never have to go into another bank with a gun in his hand.

If he had all of it. *All* of it.

But to get all of it he'd have to double-cross these three— and Tango.

He didn't worry about the three as much as he did Tango. Because Tango had friends and contacts everywhere. Eyes, ears, and gun hands. Well—not everywhere. In talking to Tango over the years, he'd learned that his threads did not reach beyond the Big Muddy and the Mississippi.

If Pug could get across the big river with the money, he'd be safe.

He would put down his roots in an eastern town and live like a country squire. He'd change his name of course, maybe even get married to help the change, and never worry about Tango again. How could Tango find him, one man among millions? Impossible.

He rolled it around in his mind, thinking about what he could do, weighing the good and the bad. He *did* worry about Tango, but the money decided him. He would never have this chance again. If he did not take it, he'd go back to knocking over small banks, taking the long chances of a bullet out of nowhere, a hasty burial in a forgotten plot . . .

So he made his plans.

They had been keeping watch at night; with so much at stake it had to be—two and a half hours on guard for each man, and then breakfast.

The third night, as they finished eating and put out the fire, Pug brought out the quart of whiskey he'd saved for snakebite.

"We're almost home and we're due a little private celebration," he said. "Drink up." He passed the quart bottle around, and they smoked and jabbered and drank.

Frank kept them in stitches with stories about some of the wild women he'd known, and Pug pretended to drink along with everyone else. And pretended to get as woozy as they. A quart was a lot of whiskey; it took two hours to finish it. Tim almost fell in the still-smoldering coals of the fire, and Lem went to sleep where he sat.

Pug got them all on their backs, dropped a blanket over each one, and saddled his horse. They were all snoring when he rode away at a walk, leading their horses. They would probably sleep till the middle of the next morning.

In the meantime he'd be too far along the way to be stopped. And he'd be rich.

Jules said, "I guess that this man, Pug, got the others drunk and left them sleeping."

"A very good guess," Ki agreed.

They set out again with Jules in the lead. Four horses left an easy trail. Bennett had doubtless left the camp at night, and had ridden in a comparatively straight line for about five miles.

When they came to a small valley, they found the three horses cropping grass.

Jules said, "It was probably getting light when he reached here. I'm sure he did not want to meet anyone while he was leading three horses. So he left them in the first convenient place."

When they went on, Jules had to get down several times to examine the ground, walking head-down sometimes for a hundred yards or more. "It's definitely daylight now, for him, and he's trying to hide his tracks just in case. That's my guess."

"You're an excellent guesser," Ki told him.

Jules smiled. "It's like old times. I haven't done this for years." He mounted his horse and, after a bit, galloped far ahead to get down and study the ground again. Then he motioned them on. Bennett had stopped trying to be clever and was making time, careless of hoofprints.

Jules said, "He probably doesn't think anyone could follow him this far."

"Where's he going?" Jessie asked.

"You want me to guess?"

"Guess," Ki said.

"To the Mississippi," Jules replied. "Nobody can track him on water. He could go up, down, or across the river."

Ki said, "We'd better catch him before he reaches it."

The tracks led directly toward a town and, reaching a road, mingled with others. Jules thought Pug might think himself safe now. He might even stay overnight.

But they found he had not slept in the hotel. He had stayed in the stable with his horse.

"He did that," Ki said, "because of the money. He has to guard it."

They took rooms in the hotel, and in the morning it took Jules a while to locate Bennett's tracks. He had tried to hide them again in the roadway that led south. He had branched off in a shallow stream that flowed from the west. Jules found where he had left the stream to go east again.

Then it rained.

It was a downpour, and they took refuge in a thick copse of pines that gave them shelter for half a day, till the deluge tapered off. Toward nightfall they came to a road and turned into it. There were no tracks to follow. The road took them into a small burg, Sheldon, where they arrived just before midnight. They woke the hotel clerk, who was sleeping on a cot behind the desk. He gave them keys and took their money, grumpy at being disturbed. He hardly looked at them.

It was still raining lightly when Jessie woke in the morning, dressed, and went downstairs. A different, much older clerk was on duty; he had just relieved the night man, he told her, round-eyed to see such a vision across the desk. What could he do for her?

She asked if he had a recent newspaper, and he scurried to find one for her, chattering like a magpie to keep her in the tiny lobby. There were so few interesting people who came to Sheldon, he said, usually only scruffy strangers passing through, like the one who had left in a hurry that very morning.

Jessie's eyes brightened. "The tall man in the black frock coat?"

"No. This one was short and red-headed. Been here since yesterday night. Mostly sleeping, I think."

He was startled when Jessie jumped and ran up the stairs like a deer. He looked after her with his mouth hanging open.

She rapped hard on Ki's door. When he opened it, she said, "Pug left here this morning."

"Damn! Get Jules up."

They saddled their horses in the stable, donned slickers against the drizzle, and rode out, heading east. Jules quickly found fresh tracks, of a horseman with the wind at his back. The mist did not erase hoofprints.

The rider was perhaps two, maybe three, hours ahead of them, Jules said.

Pug was taking his time. No one was on his trail by now. Who could track him through the rain? Trackers were damn few and far between anyway these days. Their sun had pretty much set.

He was thinking ahead to New Orleans. He ought to give himself a fling before he dug a hole and pulled it in after him. And there was nowhere a man could have a screaming, wallowing time like New Orleans. There was something about the town . . . The girls were willing and wild, and the sky was the limit. He had been to big towns, like Kansas City, and a man with money could have a good time there or in St. Louis. But no town was like New Orleans. It had a flavor . . .

The only trouble was, Tango had too many friends there. Tango had spent years in the city and still kept in contact with many of the people he knew there. But just maybe he could slip in, have his fling, and ease out again before

150

Tango could put out the word on him.

How long would it take Lem, Tim, and Frank to find horses and get back to Otillo? Then for Tango to write letters—there was no telegraph in the Strip. Someone would have to ride out to civilization with the letters; that would take a week. So it would take a month or two for Tango to alert his friends in New Orleans that Pug *might* come that way. And he might not.

It stopped raining for a time, then started up again, the dark clouds seeming just over his head, spilling water down upon him. Pug bowed his head, hunched his shoulders, and rode on at a walk. Let it rain. The raging storm was his friend. When he looked back, he could see his tracks disappearing in the muck. Lady Luck was still at his elbow.

When he came to a fork in the road, he halted and studied the choice, then decided on the left and plodded on with the rain beating on his back.

He dozed in the saddle and sometime later looked up to see a farmhouse and barn off to his right. He turned into the farm road and went to the barn at once. It was dark, and he saw no lights on in the house. He opened the door, led the horse inside, and closed it again. He scratched a match, found a lantern on a wire, and lighted the wick. He'd give the farmer a dollar in the morning.

He took the lantern to the last stall and hung it on a nail. He unsaddled the horse, gave it hay, and dumped the money out of the bags.

It was raining harder, drumming on the roof, with occasional lightning forking in the sky and the far roll of thunder like distant artillery. Pug sat down in the stall and began to count the money.

He took his time, carefully putting the various denominations in separate, neat piles, all smiles inside at the sight of so much legal tender. He stopped now and then to unfold and smooth out a bill, humming to himself. What a pleasant way to spend a few hours, counting money as it stormed outside.

He was concentrating on the job at hand—and jumped a foot, spilling a handful of tens, as a rough voice behind him spoke: "Who the hell're you?" Then the voice changed. "Jesus Christ! Lookit that!"

Pug turned, sliding his pistol out. He looked at a skinny older man who wore a soaking wet overcoat and a sopping floppy hat. The man was staring at the piles of money, his mouth a round O.

He carried a shotgun, but he was so startled by the mounds of greenbacks that he seemed paralyzed.

Pug growled at him. "Drop the shotgun."

The farmer apparently realized then that he had the gun and turned it toward Pug, who fired instantly. Three shots slammed the older man against the side of the building, where he fell, a crumpled, shapeless mass in the shadows.

Pug swore and got up to nudge the old man, but he was gone. Shit! He went to the door and looked toward the house. There was a glimmer from one of the windows. The farmer must have seen a sliver of light in the barn and come to investigate.

The man probably had a wife and kids who would come to see where the farmer had got to—sooner or later. Pug wondered if they had heard the shots. Maybe not, if it had been thundering at the moment. He saw no movement in the house.

He went back, found a grain sack, and dumped all the money into it, a sizeable load. He saddled the horse again and tied the sack on, then donned his slicker and climbed aboard, settling the skirts of the slicker over the money sack. There was no wind at all. He'd buy a carpetbag or one of those newfangled rubber sacks first chance he got.

He rode out to the road and headed east, swearing at the horse's ears. Why did the old fool have to come out just at that time to slip up behind him? But no one had seen him, he was sure. They would think some drifter had shot the farmer.

He rode all night long and half the next morning before he reached Teplar, a wide place in the road. It had a shacky little grocery, a tiny dry goods store, and a blacksmith shop that was tight closed. The rain had let up, though it was chilly; the grocer had an iron belly stove giving off welcome heat in the center of the room.

Pug bought some vittles, and a heavy bag at the dry goods store. It would turn water, the owner promised. Pug put the food in it and rode away.

In the first little woods he came to, he transferred the money to the new bag and put the vittles in the grain sack. It was some thirty miles to the next town, they had told him.

The grocer said he hoped the bridge wasn't washed out.

★

Chapter 22

The outlaw's tracks he followed faded into nothingness as the rain came down harder, pounding the road. Jules halted, pulling his poncho tighter about him. Jessie and Ki stopped beside him, and Jules said, "The tracks are gone. Shall we keep on this way?"

Jessie said, "What's your guess?"

Jules shrugged. "I don't believe he thinks he's being followed now. He's been pointing east from the start. I still think he's going to the big river." He glanced at Ki, who nodded.

Ki said, "East it is."

When they came to the fork in the road, they halted. It was raining steadily, and there were no tracks, only puddles merrily splashing. Jules scratched his chin. "I think the left fork goes a bit more to the east than the other."

Jessie asked, "Would Pug Bennett think so?"

"Why wouldn't he?"

"Then let's go left." Ki turned his horse.

Hours later the rain gradually slackened, misted awhile, then stopped altogether. The road they followed was a muddy trail with long pools of brown water snaking along it. They came to a rail fence and in the distance could make out buildings, which turned out to be a farmhouse and barn with sheds and corrals.

A group of people was standing in front of the barn, and one of them, on seeing the riders, came striding out to the road. He was a big man wearing a store suit and boots, with a silver star pinned to his breast pocket. Across the star was imprinted the word "Sheriff."

He motioned them to stop. Seeing Jessie, he touched his hat. "You folks come from quite a way over west?"

Ki replied. "Yes, we have, Sheriff. What's the trouble?"

"You meet anybody on the road?"

"No . . ."

"You positive? Nobody?"

"No one at all." There was a woman in the group who appeared to be weeping. Two young boys were with her.

The sheriff said, "Man got hisself shot last night, in the barn."

"D'you know who did it?"

"No. I figger somebody was sleepin' in the barn and Bates rousted him out and the feller shot 'im."

"Pug," Jules said.

The lawman frowned at him. "What?"

Ki said, "We're hoping to catch up with Pug Bennett. We're pretty sure he came this way."

"Bennett! Bennett's in this here neck o' the woods?"

"I'm afraid so. He might be your man." Ki nodded toward the barn. "How'd he get shot?"

"Miz Bates said he went out to the barn late last night. Thought he seen something. It was rainin' pretty hard.

Anyways, when he didn't come back, she sent one of the boys and he found the body. Shot three times." The sheriff shook his head. "Maybe he surprised Bennett— if it was Bennett—and got shot. Bennett's a killer they say."

"Yes, he is."

An undertaker's wagon arrived as they talked, and two men got down in front of the barn. On the side of the wagon was printed DR. C. LARSON, URILLA SPRINGS.

Jessie asked, "What's ahead of us, Sheriff?"

"Well, they's Teplar, about fifteen miles. It's just a couple of stores. Danville is near thirty miles. I got a deputy in Danville. I'd take it kindly if you'd tell him you seen me. I be there in a day'r two."

"Of course," Jessie said.

When they left the house behind, Ki said, "If Pug was in the barn when the farmer came and found him, why did he shoot?"

Jules said, "Like the sheriff said, he was surprised."

"Maybe so, but Pug Bennett is an experienced owlhoot. Even if he were surprised, would he shoot the farmer, knowing he couldn't stay there then? He'd pay the man, wouldn't he? The sheriff said it was raining very hard."

Jessie said, "Maybe the farmer recognized him from a poster and made the mistake of saying so."

"That's more likely!" Ki said.

"We're reasonably satisfied it *was* Pug then?" Jessie asked.

Ki nodded. "I don't doubt it very much."

"Then we're still on his trail," Jules said grimly.

When they reached Teplar, the store owner told them a man of Pug's description had been there and bought vittles. "He was a short feller . . ."

"What color hair?"

"Couldn't see his hair. It was rainin'. He was wearin' a hat."

Jessie went into the dry goods store and learned that the same man had bought a heavy, waterproof bag.

"To put the money in," she said to Ki. He agreed.

The next town, Danville, was due east over generally flat country; they rode in long after dark and put up at the hotel. No one of Pug's description was in the place, the clerk said.

The next morning Ki gave the sheriff's message to the deputy in his office. "Pug Bennett? He's in this area? Are you sure?" He appeared very nervous.

"We're sure," Ki said.

Ki visited several saloons while Jessie talked to tradesmen. They could find no one who recalled a man of Pug's description coming into town.

Pug halted, seeing the rooflines of Danville in the distance. He needed nothing in the town; there was no reason to go in. He glanced at the sky . . . plenty of daylight left and no rain.

He rode around the town, met the road again on the far side, and continued. The bridge the grocer had mentioned was intact over a swollen stream. Pug's horse clattered over it.

He was beginning to have second thoughts about New Orleans. It might be wise to go north to the Missouri River and down it to St. Louis—and stay there. Not even stop in Kansas City.

Tango was not to be taken lightly, and Tango would never forget or forgive the double-cross. He would do everything in his power to get even.

Pug sighed. If he didn't play everything very smart, he'd get a sudden shotgun blast in the back some night. The idea

157

made him shudder a bit. He wanted to go to New Orleans, but he was feeling more and more that he didn't dare. Lady Luck was whispering in his ear to watch his step. He was realizing he would have to take care the rest of his life. Between Tango and those damned posters that were up everywhere, he was a marked man.

That night, cooking over a tiny fire in a deep hole, he decided. The smart thing was to go north to the river, get on a boat somehow, and have his fling in St. Louis. It wouldn't be quite the same, but it might evade the shotgun blast. After all, Tango was a Southerner. He could not recall Tango ever mentioning anyone north of Cairo.

That settled, he curled up and slept till dawn.

Rochfort was a river town, mostly a sleepy place. The big steamboats usually passed it by, and the smaller craft nudged in with goods and a few passengers on an occasional basis. Fisher boats cluttered the inlet, and several rickety piers thrust out into the stream.

Pug looked it over from a distance and approached it by the main road just before sundown, walking his horse. He could smell the river and hear a few far-off bells and whistles. There was a big side-wheeler threshing along far out on the Big Muddy with a white wake streaming along behind her. The boat was brightly lighted, a river palace. What he would give to be aboard her!

He looked down at himself—tattered, wrinkled, and dirty. He was wearing clothes he would have thrown away long since in other times. Well, he'd correct that in a hurry. Maybe this town had a good dry goods or clothing store. He'd spend thirty or forty dollars and outfit himself.

Nudging the horse, he rode into town on a side street.

The first shot startled him. The bullet picked at his collar. Frantically he dug in spurs, turning the horse as more shots cracked by him. Who the hell was shooting?

The horse ran flat out into the dark, over a slight rise and into some scrawny woods. Yanking his Winchester out of its scabbard, he reined in and slid down. He rested the barrel on the saddle, watching the road. Had Tango put the word out on him already? It *had* to be Tango. Jesus, he must be offering a wad of money!

No one came along the road.

Pug chewed his lower lip. Probably this bushwhacker knew the country. Was there a better way to get at him? Was there only one of them?

He'd go around the town then and go south to the next town to find a boat. Mounting the horse, he turned left, the rifle across his thighs. He had gone perhaps a hundred feet when a shot slammed into the tree beside him, showering him with bits of bark. Son of a bitch!

The shot had come from his left. He turned right and ducked low. It was too dark for accurate shooting in the woods. The sniper had probably heard the hoofbeats and fired at the sound. But how had this one gotten so far so soon?

There were two of them!

He turned into the road and galloped west as if the devil himself were chasing. A shot followed, but far off the mark. He was probably invisible in the dark now. The shot was just anger.

Had Tango outguessed him?

Pug groaned. He had doubtless opened his big mouth in Tango's presence, talking about the wild times he'd had in New Orleans. So Tango had wired everyone he knew along the river, probably offering big cash for Bennett's head . . . to say nothing of the reward.

Pug groaned aloud, feeling like a fool. Of course, that was it. Tango had eyes and ears everywhere; he constantly paid money for information. His network of listeners was extensive; he had built it up over many years. It was the base for all his plans.

He hadn't taken Tango seriously enough.

Pug slowed the horse after several miles and halted off the road. He could hear no one following. He sat, listening, and heard only an owl, hooting over and over again. Maybe the snipers hadn't followed him.

But if Tango was offering enough, plus the reward, why wouldn't they follow? Maybe they knew another way.

He moved on, walking the horse on the grass at the side of the road, heading west. Maybe he'd be able to make a big circle and reach the river at another point. Or—maybe he'd go on west to San Francisco! He'd thought of that many times, and Tango might not expect it.

He halted after a few miles and listened again. Still nothing. Stepping down, he led the horse into the trees and unsaddled. He chewed dried meat, his back to a tree, the rifle across his thighs, a round in the chamber.

★

Chapter 23

Pug Bennett's trail led to the town of Rochfort—but not into it. The hoofprints halted abruptly at the edge of town, on a side street opposite a blacksmith shop, then retreated, the horse at a gallop.

Jules examined the street, walking here and there, "Something happened here—maybe a fight." He peered at the blacksmith shop. "Maybe he saw it . . ."

Jessie got down and entered the shop with him. The smith, a big man with a leather apron over bare, bronzed shoulders, turned and stared at Jessica in surprise. "Howdy, ma'am . . ."

She gave him her best smile and explained what they wanted. The smith nodded. "I heard them shots and looked out. They was two fellers shootin'." He walked to the front of the shop and pointed. "I seen 'em over by the bakery there. The hombre they was shootin' at went thataway fast as he could go." He pointed west. "He a friend o'yours?"

"We know him," Jessie said. "Do you think he was hit?"

161

"Didn't look like it. Bad light for shootin'."

"When did it happen?"

"Last night, early, just about dark."

Jessie asked, "What about the two men? Did they chase him?"

"I dunno. They run back along the buildin' there and out of my sight. But I'd guess they did."

They thanked the smith and went out to the horses.

The tracks of a galloping horse lay along the side of the road, occasionally on the grass at its side. In a short while Jules reined in.

"Here's where he stopped—probably to see if he was being followed. He got down and waited awhile. He must have been surprised to be shot at that way."

Jessie looked at Ki. "Who was doing the shooting?"

"Citizens after the reward?"

"Is that likely? How would they know he was coming into town?"

"Then he was expected . . . ?"

"Yes, but how?"

Jules said, "He went on west, keeping over to the side of the road close to the trees."

After a few miles Jules halted again. "He stopped here and stayed here for a bit. Maybe he heard something." He went back to the road. "Then he went on slow—walking his horse in the grass, being quiet."

Several miles farther Jules halted again, got down, and walked off the road. When he came back he said, "He spent the night here . . . cold camp."

Jessie asked, "Why is Pug Bennett, a gunslick and killer, a longtime outlaw, running from two snipers?"

Jules smiled at her. "Because he's carrying a fortune in cash. One lucky shot from them and he'd never enjoy a penny of it. He's just being careful and smart."

"You think like an owlhoot, Jules," Ki said.

Jules sighed. "I was one once."

Pug was far off the road, heading north and west. The land was rolling, with clumps of trees and a woods here and there. He halted in each copse of trees and searched the land with his eyes. There were two of them coming after him, and once he'd glimpsed one, far off to his left, too far to see details.

Maybe neither was a tracker and they were guessing about where he might be. And he was wary and alert. He owned so much money! It excited him just to contemplate it. And he was raging inside that they were keeping him from his future.

Distance was what he needed. Distance from them. They had turned him away from the river; he must be miles and miles from it now. He frowned, wondering where the second man was now. Damn! He wished he had Tipo or Bob with him, or good old Windy, who seldom put more than two words together at a time.

It was beginning to mist. Heavy fog was drifting along just overhead, and it was turning colder. He rode into a small woods and walked the horse through it, then halted just inside the line of trees and peered off to his right. Was there movement a half mile away—a man, or maybe a deer? He'd seen a lot of deer.

It was a deer, bursting from the far trees suddenly, running like the wind toward the east.

That meant there was a man in those trees!

Pug eased away to the south, still in the woods, and fingered his rifle. If he could entice one of the them into an ambush, he'd even the odds.

But they were both wary of closing with him, evidently respecting his reputation. They'd probably stay at rifle range if they could—and wear him down.

Did they know about the money he had? Maybe that was why they were so persistent. Probably their plan was to wear him down by keeping him awake, tiring him out. But that would work against them too.

Late in the day he came out onto the open prairie, and now he saw them more often. But when he deliberately rode toward one, the man turned away.

Pug halted on a brushy rise at dusk. The land rolled away on four sides. He and the horse were concealed from the pursuer's sight, but they knew where he was . . . and they began shooting at the rise from long distance.

He made the horse lie down, and he returned the fire, shooting at muzzle flashes, but unable to tell where his shots were landing. Most of theirs fell short.

The firing stopped when darkness came. He wondered if they would try to crawl close . . . He chewed dried meat and listened. And listened.

The firing had come from widely separated spots. Toward morning, when it was darkest, he led the horse down one slope, moving west. He walked very slowly, a pistol in his hand. With any luck he would pass between them.

He had gone several hundred yards when a shot came suddenly from his left and slammed into the dirt a short distance behind him. Someone had fired at the sounds. Pug halted, holstered the Colt, and drew the rifle from its scabbard. When the next shot came, he fired at the muzzle blast five times, as fast as he could work the lever.

Then silence.

Had he hit one of them? He mounted the horse and went on more quickly.

Jules lost the tracks and halted. "He didn't come this way." He turned the horse, went back, dismounted, and walked along, peering at the ground. It took nearly an hour before he found the place where Bennett had left the road.

"He's a long way from the river," Ki said. "They seem to be herding him west."

"They're certainly trying to keep him from the river," Jules agreed. "If he ever got on it, they could lose him for good."

The going was very slow, with Jules walking, leading his horse. Many times he halted and shook his head in despair. He could not be sure, he confessed, if they were on Pug's trail or not. He had not seen a clear print for hours.

They halted when night fell, and Ki dug a deep pit for a small fire. Jules walked away from the camp and came back in a hurry. "I hear firing . . ."

On the top of a low, rounded hill they could hear shots in the distance. "Maybe they've treed him," Jessie said.

Ki suggested they move closer. "How far away are the shots, would you say?"

"Several miles. Sound carries in the night," Jules said.

The firing stopped before they had gone very far. When it stopped, they halted and Ki said, "Let's not rush in. It might be better if we wait till morning."

But daylight showed them very little. When they rode to the place the shooting had come from, they found empty brass on the ground but nothing else.

"A lot of shooting and probably no result," Ki said. "The snipers hoped to get lucky."

Jessie shaded her eyes, looking westward. "And Pug got away from them."

Pug rode steadily the rest of the night, hearing nothing further from the pursuit. Toward morning he came upon a natural fort, a bit of broken land that provided a dozen excellent rifle pits. It crowned a low rise of ground and had a depression in its center that was grassy. He hobbled the horse and crawled into one of the pits with the Winchester, and waited.

His position was difficult to spot, slightly higher than the approach. He hadn't seen it himself until he'd been almost atop it. A perfect ambush point.

The smoldering anger against these two was burning inside him. They had smashed his plans and they'd been able to do it because of the money. Now that he had a fortune in his grasp, he wanted to take no chances. One stray bullet could knock his future into a cocked hat.

He wished for a pair of binoculars. Was that a horseman far off to the right, a dot on the land? He squinted and decided it probably was a man. The object disappeared and reappeared much closer. It was a man on a sorrel horse.

The other sniper should have been somewhere to his left, but Pug could see no trace of him. The two of them were probably searching for a sign of him, and Pug smiled, sliding the rifle out and sighting along it. The man on the sorrel was still out of rifle range; he was leaning down, examining the ground as he moved along slowly. As he came closer, Pug could see that he wore blue Levi pants, a checked shirt, and an old brown coat. He had a battered dark hat and was probably a hardcase, hired by someone in Tango's debt.

Pug laid the rifle sights on the distant rider and waited patiently, watching the other man come closer and closer . . .

Then he was within range. Long range. Pug hugged the Winchester to his shoulder and drew back the hammer. He put the front sight on the man's middle and followed along; his finger caressed the trigger . . .

Now he took up the trigger slack, let his breath out, took a long breath, and held it—and began to squeeze.

When the rifle fired, the rider toppled from the saddle. He fell like a sack of grain and never moved again. The sorrel pranced sideways in surprise, then halted, shaking its head.

Pug did not move. He looked for the second man—had he heard the shot? If so, would he come to investigate? Pug smiled, hoping to get both of them. He remained motionless, drawing the barrel back so it could not be seen, in case the other man had a spyglass.

But the second man did not show up.

Pug waited more than an hour—then he heard a peculiar whistle. It came from somewhere in front of him, maybe off a bit to the left . . . It was sustained and had a curious warble. It came two or three times, then faded away. It was probably a signal, he decided. That the whistler's partner would never answer.

As he stood up and stretched, he noticed a speck of movement far to the right, and in a moment made out the shapes of three riders.

Jesus! How many were after him!?

It must be the reward money—or did everyone know by now about the seventy-plus thousand? If so, that was enough to turn out the entire population of Kansas! They would pick his bones clean.

He hurried to the waiting horse, tightened the cinch, and mounted. He'd best go west, put distance between him and them, all of them, then maybe find a place to hole up for a while, till the hue and cry died down. Sooner or later his Wanted posters would be plastered over by others and he'd be forgotten . . .

What a difference, now that he had a fortune. That day could not come too soon.

• • •

Jules lost the tracks on the prairie sod and shook his head in defeat.

"I would know the tracks of his horse if I saw them again . . ." He shrugged. "But the chance of running onto them is not good."

"We ought to continue west," Ki said. "That's the way he was going."

"And hope to find tracks," Jessie agreed.

They went slowly, wary of every fold of ground that might hide a sniper, but they saw no one in the vast emptiness of the plains. They were the center of a great formless sea that swirled around them as the breezes moved the prairie grass so that the land seemed to breathe.

It rained again, and they took shelter under trees where there was plenty of firewood. Toward morning the first snow settled down, silent as thought, a light dusting that barely stayed on the ground.

After a meager breakfast they went on for half a day, till Jules pointed into the distance. "Is that a column of smoke?"

Jessie put the binoculars on it. "Yes, it is. Someone doesn't worry about raiders."

"Maybe it's an army fort," Ki said.

But in two hours they saw it was a large stone hut, as good as a fort. It had rifle ports and a thick roof where weeds grew around the chimney in its center.

"It's a trader," Jules said. He rode toward the hut and yelled.

A big man appeared in the doorway with a shotgun in his arms. He was bearded and dressed in buckskins, and he looked them over carefully. Finally he beckoned them to come on and pointed to the corral beside the hut.

His name was painted on a board nailed over the door: J. SPARKS. PROP. WE TRADE.

They put the animals into the corral and went inside to introduce themselves. J. Sparks stared at Jessie in undisguised admiration.

"I ain't seen a white woman in three, four years!" He gazed round at them. "You folks lost?"

Ki shook his head, and Jessie said, "We're looking for a man, Pug Bennett. He's wanted for half a dozen crimes."

"You all the law?"

"No, but we'll take him in."

"Never heard of 'im," J. Sparks said, making a face. He put half a log into the big black stove in the middle of the room and slammed the iron door. The room was lined with shelves that sagged with piles of skins and various articles. Its smell was heavy.

Sparks said eagerly, "You got a newspaper? What's goin' on out there in civilization?"

"The war's over . . ."

"Yeah, I know that. And I heard somebody shot ol' Abe. That was a while ago. You hear anything about Ohio?"

Nobody had. Nor had they a newspaper. Sparks said he'd seen one several years past when a visitor had given him part of one that had been wrapped around some fish.

He told them his hut was smack-dab on an ancient Indian trail leading north and south. He'd been trading with his Red brothers for a lot of years.

But now he was getting on, and thinking of returning to Ohio, to one of the corn counties where he'd been born. He wanted to see if any of his relations and friends were still alive. He was alone now, his wife having died nine years past.

They stayed overnight at the hut and continued west in the forenoon. It was an auspicious day; the sun came out

169

and warmed the land, but by nightfall the clouds were rolling in again from the northwest, dark and threatening. It did not rain or snow for two days, and the ground dried a bit.

They met a dozen people—men, women and a few shirttail-size children—at a river crossing, but none had seen a man of Pug's description.

They followed the river for several days and came to Elroy at a ford and on a stageline. It was a seedy little town, grown up about the stage station, and they found the posters of Pug Bennett plastered over with those of Dirty Bill Sands. But there was no picture of him.

They were able to get baths at a public bathhouse and rooms at a hotel-boardinghouse. They slept in real beds and ate in one of the two restaurants.

The town marshal seemed very edgy when Ki told him that Pug Bennett was possibly heading his way.

★

Chapter 24

Pug did not see the second sniper again. Maybe, at the death of his partner, he had decided to call it quits. But, though Pug did not see the man, he could not be sure he'd gone. It was necessary to take all precautions.

He waited for nightfall and continued west, into the wind. It should not be difficult to find a place where he could spend the winter quietly, where no one would accost him. Maybe he would locate a small house on the edge of some town or other and hole up. He'd tell the neighbors, if they were nosy, some story to account for his presence, and send a boy now and then for vittles.

It would be lonely for a time, but the months would go by as they always did, and then he'd go to the river again. By that time all the hue and cry would have died down and no one would be looking for him.

The more he thought about it, the better it sounded. The big drawback was going to be the loneliness. He would have to put up with it, then he'd be free. Even Tango would have to give up the vendetta, figuring he'd gone far east—or had died.

He considered writing to a Kansas City newspaper—all the Western papers picked up items from them—saying that he had been with Pug Bennett when Pug had cashed in his chips after a prairie fight. He would tell how he'd buried Pug . . . Would they believe it? Or would they see through it, wanting more confirmation?

He sighed deeply. Probably it was too transparent. It might only put his name back in the papers when he wanted them to forget him.

The best thing was his original idea, to disappear. He'd change his name, get some other clothes, and act like a retired shopkeeper. Could he do that? Just for the winter?

Of course he could.

He noticed smoke on the southern horizon—that seemed to move. Maybe it was a train. He went that way and found iron rails and a telegraph line. He followed the tracks and came to a little burg—too small for his purpose. It had no store and was only a few scattered houses where railroad workers lived.

He passed it by and two days later came to Tenspot, a bright, new little place on a shallow stream. It was the end of the track, with a roundhouse and sheds, half a dozen saloons and stores, and, best of all, a red light district. There were about a dozen houses, all catering to the railroad men.

Pug waited for dark before entering the town, and then went directly to the district and put his horse in one of the house stables. He hid the money sacks under a pile of hay in the stall and went into the house.

Three girls were available in the parlor, and he chose one who said her name was Helen. He was dirty and bedraggled; he hadn't shaved for many days, but apparently she was used to men in that condition and helped him pull his boots off.

She turned the lamp wick low and slid out of her loose dress to shake her boobies at him. Then she lay on the bed, and he climbed atop her at once in a terrible hurry.

She guided him and said, "You ain't had it for a time, huh?"

"I been out in the sticks."

"Yeah, you sure have." She slapped his bare rump. "Come git it, honey."

The stores were closed when he left the house, so he camped at the edge of town, by the stream. In the morning he came in as the owner unlocked the grocery door. He bought airtights and cheese, which he was partial to, and left the town behind, moving west.

The next town, the grocer had told him, was the county seat, near thirty miles due west.

The road curved gently toward the south, and a line of sketchy, low hills moved up slowly from the horizon. He reached the town well after dark, tired and hungry. He camped beside a small stream, where many others had camped before him, and ate near-cold beans from a can. The county seat probably housed the sheriff and maybe some deputies—a lot of law in one place. He would be smart to slide out early and keep going.

But in the morning, as he prepared to hit the road, Binder came along. He had been camping not far away, he said. His name was Nate Binder and he had a gold tooth in front.

"I seen you in Otillo. You're Pug Bennett." He grinned and the tooth gleamed. "Tango said you was the best."

"You know Tango?"

"Hell yeah. Had many a romp with his girls."

"What you doing here?"

173

"Stayin' out of sight." Binder had a horse and blanket roll and apparently nothing else. "I didn' know this was the county seat when I come in. They's a damn courthouse over there." He pointed. "Too goddam much law t'suit me." He glanced at the saddlebags. "You headin' west?"

Pug said, "Thought I'd go back to the Strip."

"Suits me. Mind if I ride along?"

Pug shrugged. He could hardly say no. He didn't want the company, and he didn't recall ever seeing Binder in Otillo. Binder was maybe forty, lean and bedraggled as himself, very obviously down on his luck and probably looking for a way to overcome that drawback.

He felt a sudden suspicion that Binder had come along at this particular time; could he be working for Tango? No, probably not. How could anyone suspect he'd be here in this spot? Binder was probably just drifting.

But he had quick eyes for the saddlebags.

Pug did not turn his back to Binder at any time and kept him to the left. If Binder noticed, he said nothing.

They left the town behind. The road, fringed by scant bunchgrass, wound through low, brushy hills. Binder chattered, saying he'd been up to the north, looking for possibilities and finding few.

"Not too much a man can do alone. Had a partner last year, but when we hit Otillo, he went on south. Said he had kin down along the border."

"That so . . ." Pug said.

"I see you ain't got a partner either."

"Don't need one. I'm retired this year." Pug said the first thing that came into his head. "Thinkin' of getting hitched."

Binder eyed the saddlebags. "You got a woman stashed somewheres?"

"In Otillo."

"Yeah? I was married once—long time ago, when I was about twenty. But I was gone a lot of time and one day I come home and she had packed up and skedaddled. Never did see 'er again."

"That so . . ." Pug said.

They camped in the hills that night, heating meat and beans over a tiny fire. After a smoke, Pug rolled up his blankets and pretended to sleep. The fire went out.

When he opened his eyes a slit, he could see Binder staring at him.

He decided to part with the other man, one way or another.

Jules decided to head for home. He was unable to do them any particular good now, he said. Pug Bennett might have gone in any direction at all and might even be holed up somewhere for the winter.

He wished them luck; they said their good-byes, and he turned back.

Both Jessie and Ki felt discouraged. There were probably dozens of towns in a hundred-mile circle around them, and Pug might be in any one of them, sitting by a fire with friends.

Ki spread out the map, but they could not tell from it even where they were. It was almost useless, not detailed, and the distances were much too inaccurate. No one had yet surveyed this far land, and maybe no one ever would.

They continued toward the setting sun.

Two days later they rode into Hatfield. Marshal Leon Hacker was astonished and delighted to see them again. "Where did you two drop from?"

"We were chasing Pug Bennett—and we lost him." Jessie related how they had followed Bennett toward the river, until he suddenly turned from it, pursued by two snipers.

175

"He could be anywhere by now," Ki said, "and carrying a huge amount of cash from the mine robbery."

Hacker nodded. "You two have been out in the sticks, so you haven't heard. The mine is offering five thousand in cash for the recovery of that money. Bennett is worth a fortune to somebody." He shrugged. "Pug is liable to get hisself shot in the back."

Jessie said, "He knew the odds when he started robbing banks. How can anyone be very sympathetic toward him?"

"It ain't sympathy he needs," Hacker replied. "It's a rope."

He was careful as hell with Binder, never turning his back for an instant. And he was sure that Binder was aware of his vigilance by now. He noted the sidelong glances and Binder's immense curiosity about the saddlebags where the money was packed. Especially since Pug slept with them under his head.

Did Binder know about the mine robbery? Maybe. Maybe not. But he was certainly broke, needing cash. Would Binder dare tangle with him?

Pug knew his mere reputation kept various hardcases at bay, not wishing to try their luck. When facing a gunslick like Pug, a man ought not to have sweaty hands. Any tiny mistake could be fatal, and Binder knew it.

But he was positive Pug carried a wad of money, else why was he so cautious? The saddlebags bulged in a most provocative manner, and Pug never opened them. They did not contain food . . . or any other supplies. He knew that Pug had taken the bank at Tannerville; probably part of the loot was in those bags.

Pug decided he would shed Binder at the next town. He would either slide out in the middle of the night without him, or simply tell him to go his own way.

And then he relaxed his guard for a second. They had just gotten down to water the horses and fill canteens in a little creek, and he turned his back.

He heard the quick click-clack as Binder drew back the hammer, and Pug ducked and rolled, snaking out his own Colt.

Binder's shot showered him with sand, and Pug fired three times, seeing dust fly off the other man's shirtfront. Binder sagged and fell heavily, half in and half out of the water, which flowed red.

Pug got up and dragged the body out, but could do nothing else. He had no tool to bury the late and slow Nate Binder, so he left him and shut his mind to the event.

He had gotten rid of Binder, not as he'd intended, but permanently, which was as well. He continued on his way and met no one for the next three days.

He was hungry. His stomach growled and he was ravenous. He had long ago emptied the sack of the airtights he'd bought, and finished the cheese. He needed a wagon train or a town with a grocery store. He saw neither on the horizon.

He went on and met no one for the next several days.

Then he shot a rabbit and skinned it. He broiled bits over a fire and ate like a starving man. It kept him in the saddle till he saw a town in the distance.

When he arrived everything but the saloons was closed. He investigated the rear of the general store. His hands were shaking from hunger when he broke the window and crawled in.

He did not see the ragged man, sleeping under a pile of boxes, who woke at the sound, wondering what he had heard. Manny was sober, having slept off his latest drunk. He felt awful; his skin crawled and, being sober, he had a terrible taste in his mouth. He crawled out of the hideaway and managed to stand up.

Then he saw the broken store window.

Blinking, he moved to it unsteadily and peered in. There was a man in the store with the light off. Probably a burglar!

If he gave the alarm, someone or two were sure to buy him drinks! The store owner would certainly give him money as a reward . . . He hurried around the building to the street and pounded on Marshal Hacker's door.

Hacker, Jessie, and Ki converged on the general store building. The three had been sitting in the marshal's office talking when Manny showed up. Hacker went around to the back and yelled in the broken window for the thief to come out.

Startled, Pug fired at the sound, then ran to the front door and unfastened the chains. He opened the door to the dark street and stepped out, the revolver in his hand.

There was a blond woman standing in the street facing him, with a slim, dark man near her.

The blonde and the Chinaman! Jesus! They had tracked him down!

But the Chinaman had no gun. Pug smiled and raised the pistol, thumbing back the hammer—and saw a flash of light! His mind told him in a split instant that it was the same kind of lightning he'd seen when Bob died.

It was the last thing he saw.

Men brought lanterns and held them high over the body as Ki retrieved the *shuriken*.

"It's Pug Bennett!" Hacker said in astonishment. "What's he doing, robbing a grocery store?"

Ki pointed to the cracker crumbs on the dead man's coat. "He was hungry."

They found Pug's horse behind the store and saddlebags packed with money that belonged to the mine.

"He had all this money," Jessie said, "but he had to break into the store because he was hungry."

"There's a message there somewhere," Ki said.

Watch for

LONE STAR AND THE WOLF PACK

125th in the exciting LONE STAR series
from Jove

Coming in January!

A special offer for people who enjoy reading the best Westerns published today.

WESTERNS!

NO OBLIGATION

Mail the coupon below

To start your subscription and receive 2 FREE WESTERNS, fill out the coupon below and mail it today. We'll send your first shipment which includes 2 FREE BOOKS as soon as we receive it.

Mail To: **True Value Home Subscription Services, Inc. P.O. Box 5235**
120 Brighton Road, Clifton, New Jersey 07015-5235

YES! I want to start reviewing the very best Westerns being published today. Send me my first shipment of 6 Westerns for me to preview FREE for 10 days. If I decide to keep them, I'll pay for just 4 of the books at the low subscriber price of $2.75 each; a total $11.00 (a $21.00 value). Then each month I'll receive the 6 newest and best Westerns to preview Free for 10 days. If I'm not satisfied I may return them within 10 days and owe nothing. Otherwise I'll be billed at the special low subscriber rate of $2.75 each; a total of $16.50 (at least a $21.00 value) and save $4.50 off the publishers price. There are never any shipping, handling or other hidden charges. I understand I am under no obligation to purchase any number of books and I can cancel my subscription at any time, no questions asked. In any case the 2 FREE books are mine to keep.

Name
_____

Street Address _____ Apt. No. _____

City _____ State _____ Zip Code _____

Telephone _____

Signature _____
(if under 18 parent or guardian must sign)

Terms and prices subject to change. Orders subject
to acceptance by True Value Home Subscription
Services. Inc.

10998